The Torrents of Spring

Ernest Miller Hemingway was born in 1899. His father was a doctor and he was the second of six children. Their home was at Oak Park, a Chicago suburb.

In 1917 Hemingway joined the Kansas City *Star* as a cub reporter. The following year he volunteered to work as an ambulance driver on the Italian front where he was badly wounded but twice decorated for his services. He returned to America in 1919 and married in 1921. In 1922 he reported on the Greco-Turkish war, then two years later resigned from journalism to devote himself to fiction. He settled in Paris where he renewed his earlier friendship with such fellow-American expatriates as Ezra Pound and Gertrude Stein. Their encouragement and criticism were to play a valuable part in the formation of his style.

Hemingway's first two published works were *Three Stories and Ten Poems* and *In Our Time*, but it was the satirical novel, *The Torrents of Spring*, which established his name more widely. His international reputation was firmly secured by his next three books: *Fiesta*, *Men Without Women* and *A Farewell to Arms*.

He was passionately involved with bullfighting, big-game hunting and deep-sea fishing, and his writing reflected this. He visited Spain during the Civil War and described his experiences in the bestseller, *For Whom the Bell Tolls*.

His direct and deceptively simple style of writing spawned generations of imitators but no equals. Recognition of his position in contemporary literature came in 1954 when he was awarded the Nobel Prize for Literature, following the publication of *The Old Man and the Sea*.

Ernest Hemingway died in 1961.

By the same author

Novels
Fiesta
A Farewell to Arms
To Have and Have Not
For Whom the Bell Tolls
Across the River and into the Trees
The Old Man and the Sea
Islands in the Stream
The Garden of Eden
True at First Light

Stories
Men Without Women
Winner Take Nothing
The Snows of Kilimanjaro

General
Death in the Afternoon
Green Hills of Africa
A Moveable Feast
The Dangerous Summer

Drama
The Fifth Column

Collected Works
The Essential Hemingway
The First Forty-Nine Stories
By-Line

ernest hemingway

The Torrents of Spring

A Romantic Novel in Honor of the Passing of a Great Race

And perhaps there is one reason why a comic writer should of all others be the least excused for deviating from nature, since it may not be always so easy for a serious poet to meet with the great and the admirable; but life everywhere furnishes an accurate observer with the ridiculous.

HENRY FIELDING

arrow books

Reissued in the United Kingdom by Arrow Books in 2006

14

First published in the United Kingdom in 1964 by Jonathan Cape
This edition first published in paperback in 1994 by Arrow Books

Arrow Books
The Random House Group Limited
20 Vauxhall Bridge Road, London, SW1V 2SA

Addresses for companies within The Random House Group Limited
can be found at: www.randomhouse.co.uk/offices.htm

The Random House Group Limited Reg. No. 954009

www.randomhouse.co.uk

A CIP catalogue record for this book is available from the British Library

ISBN 9780099909507

Typeset by SX Composing DTP, Rayleigh, Essex

Penguin Random House is committed to a sustainable future for
our business, our readers and our planet. This book is made from
Forest Stewardship Council® certified paper.

Printed and bound in Great Britain by Clays Ltd, St Ives plc

Contents

To H. L. Mencken and
S. Stanwood Mencken

In Admiration

Introduction

Thirty-one years ago when I read *The Torrents of Spring* and wrote an introduction to it, I thought it was screamingly funny. I do not think it so very funny now. The reason is that the literary approach and style which Hemingway was parodying had imposed itself on us then and we were delighted to find it ridiculed. Now the joke needs explanation, so that it has lost its topical point. On the other hand, it is more interesting than when it was written because Hemingway has turned out to be a much greater writer than anyone would have guessed when he wrote *The Torrents of Spring,* and it tells us a good deal about his development.

It was his second book, written when he was an almost penniless writer living in Paris, happily in love with his first wife, but seeing a great deal of literary society. The impressions of those formative years are now available to us in *A Moveable Feast,* an all-too-short piece of posthumous autobiography. From that book one can see how greatly his literary dealings and friendships with Gertrude Stein, Ford Madox Ford and Scott Fitzgerald exasperated him. It was of this period that he wrote in the first pages of *Death in the Afternoon:*

> I was trying to write then and I found the greatest difficulty, aside from knowing what you really felt, rather that what you were supposed to feel, and had been taught to feel, was to put down what really happened in action; what the actual things were which produced the emotion that you experienced . . .
>
> I was trying to learn to write beginning with the simplest things, and one of the simplest things of all and the most fundamental is violent death . . .

It is easy to see how, for a man as serious and first-hand as that, the literary pundits of Paris would be maddening. He was desperately trying to write, he was eager to learn, but he soon realized that literary advice and literary gossip were no help to him. The only test was that every word he put down had to be honest. Moreover he was very poor, and he wrote very slowly, and the gossipers took up a lot of his time. So this parody, though it is humorous, was written with a good deal of exasperation. He had turned against his teachers.

Hemingway's first book, a collection of fine stories called *In Our Time*, was published in 1925. He had a great admiration for Sherwood Anderson when he wrote those stories and was a good deal under his influence, and Anderson, who was at the height of his fame, contributed to the blurb on the cover of

Hemingway's book. Anderson's next book *Dark Laughter* was, however, too much for Hemingway to swallow, and he reacted violently against Anderson's ideas. The following sentences taken from the first chapter of *Dark Laughter,* which describes two workmen looking out of a window into a factory yard, may indicate why.

Time very soon to push the windows up. Spring would be coming soon now . . . Sponge chewed tobacco and had a wife who got drunk with him sometimes on paydays . . . When he spoke of the other child, playfully called Bugs Martin, Sponge got a little upset. She had been a rip-terror right from the start. No doing anything with her. You couldn't keep her away from the boys. Sponge tried and his wife tried, but what good did it do? Sponge's old woman was all right. When she and Sponge were out that way after catfish and they had both taken five or six drinks of 'moon' she was like a kid . . . When the old woman was a little lit up and acted like a kid, it made Sponge feel that way too.

Later on Hemingway succumbed to the temptation to do that sort of thing himself, but the affectation of *Dark Laughter* produced a revulsion and he wrote his high-spirited parody in a few days. It was published as his second book in 1925, soon after his first.

The closest part of the parody is naturally at the opening and the reader will not be kept long before he recognizes Sponge Martin, his sporty old wife, and the playful daughter Bugs. It is not the story, however, that Hemingway is parodying, nor even the literary method, but the ideas behind it and the falsity of the author's approach to it.

Dark Laughter is the story of a newspaper reporter who leaves his highbrow wife, gets work painting wheels in a wheel-factory and draws upon himself the intentions of his boss's wife, whom he inspires with the 'same subtle desires' as she once felt for a man in Paris. She engages him as the gardener.

The motif of 'Spring was coming on in Southern Indiana' runs through *Dark Laughter,* and symbolizes and marches side by side with the slow coming together of Bruce, the workman, and his boss's wife, whose subtle desires are at length assuaged. Unfortunately a pace which appears rapid to the gardener watching asparagus in its bed agonizingly slow when we are watching the gardener himself, and the reader wearies of this vegetable love which, if it does not grow 'vaster than empires', seems to arise as slowly.

Meanwhile, below stairs, the Negro women in the house watched and waited. Often they looked at each other and giggled. 'The air on the hilltop was filled with laughter, dark laughter.' The slowness of the lady and the gardener seemed to them highly ridiculous, as it certainly would have done to more sophisticated spectators. But the Negroes, who in Hemingway are replaced by Indians, are more than Negroes, and their laughter is more than hysterical irritation with their mistress. They are children of Nature; their laughter is the voice of Nature. It is characteristic of Anderson (and of a whole school of other loose thinkers) to assume that Negroes must be nearer to Nature than white men are, and that black is a more natural colour for the skin than white.

In a brilliant critical essay Wyndham Lewis analysed in detail the ideas underlying Anderson's *Dark Laughter*, and compared them with Lawrence's ideas in *Morning in Mexico*. Nothing could be better than Wyndham Lewis's exposure of the stupidity of these ideas, and the pains-taking reader would do well to look up *Paleface*. The only fault to be found with Lewis is that he was an alarmist who saw a deadly danger lurking round every corner. But I myself cannot see in Anderson's ideas, or in Mencken's, anything very original. The view of the superiority of the child of Nature, whether he is a Negro, or a Red Indian, or a Russian peasant, dates back beyond Tolstoy, Wordsworth, Rousseau and Bernardin de St Pierre. The same idea is to be found in *Daphnis and Chloe,* and even in Genesis. It is really no more than the belief that one can find a last surviving corner of the golden age lurking on some island, or in some primitive community. And after all sometimes one can.

'Silly American painters! They chase a Gauguin shadow to the South Seas!' wrote Anderson, who found his golden age among the American Negroes. Finding a golden age, wherever it may be located, seems to me a healthy form of sport and no more likely to result in racial decadence than Hemingway's own passion for hunting and fishing. Just as it is the happy fortune of the Present to be always able to invest the Past with whatever romantic glamour it sees fit, so it is the privilege of civilized town-dwellers to sentimentalize 'primitive' peoples. No doubt they did it in Babylon. Both habits appear to be healthy and normal.

Though Anderson appears to have adopted them occasionally, D. H. Lawrence's ideas were different, more original and more personal. The Mexican Indian appealed to him for reasons which are clearly different from those which led Wordsworth to idealize the simple English cottager. It was not the virtuous golden age that Lawrence wanted; what he thought he found in the Indian and was always praising was the absence of ideas and of cerebral sex-consciousness. I am one of the few who think that his long novels would often have been better if he could have practised what he preached, as indeed he did in many of his short stories.

I mention Lawrence only because several American critics have seen a satire on Lawrence as well as on Anderson in *The Torrents of Spring*. It may be so, but I have not been able to see it. Of course Anderson is not the only subject of attack. That dear old gas-bag Ford Madox Ford proved hard for Hemingway to take, and the tales from Ford to be found here are matched by others *in A Moveable Feast*. They will delight all who knew him. Surely an anthology of anecdotes about or by Ford should be collected while there are still people alive who remember and liked or suffered from him?

The chief interest now in *The Torrents of Spring*

therefore seems to me not that it is funny, not that it is a parody of Sherwood Anderson and of his clumsily expressed ideas, but that it was a rejection by Hemingway of his teachers and literary advisers, and as such throws light on his subsequent work.

DAVID GARNETT

PART ONE

Red and Black Laughter

The only source of the true Ridiculous (as it appears to me) is affectation.

HENRY FIELDING

Chapter 1

Yogi Johnson stood looking out of the window of a big pump-factory in Michigan. Spring would soon be here. Could it be that what this writing fellow Hutchinson had said, 'If winter comes can spring be far behind?' would be true again this year? Yogi Johnson wondered. Near Yogi at the next window but one stood Scripps O'Neil, a tall, lean man with a tall, lean face. Both stood and looked out at the empty yard of the pump-factory. Snow covered the crated pumps that would soon be shipped away. Once the spring should come and the snow melt, workmen from the factory would break out the pumps from piles where they were snowed in and haul them down to the G.R. & I. station, where they would be loaded on flat-cars and shipped away. Yogi Johnson looked out of the window at the snowed-in pumps, and his breath made little fairy tracings on the cold windowpane. Yogi Johnson thought of Paris. Perhaps it was the little fairy tracings that reminded him of the gay city where he had once spent two weeks. Two weeks that were to have been the happiest weeks of his life. That was all behind him now. That and everything else.

Scripps O'Neil had two wives. As he looked out of the window, standing tall and lean and resilient with his own tenuous hardness, he thought of both of them. One lived in Mancelona and the other lived in Petoskey. He had not seen the wife who lived in Mancelona since last spring. He looked out at the snow-covered pump-yards and thought what spring would mean. With his wife in Mancelona Scripps often got drunk. When he was drunk he and his wife were happy. They would go down together to the railway station and walk out along the tracks, and sit together and drink and watch the trains go by. They would sit under a pine-tree on a little hill that overlooked the railway and drink. Sometimes they drank all night. Sometimes they drank for a week at a time. It did them good. It made Scripps strong.

Scripps had a daughter whom he playfully called Lousy O'Neil. Her real name was Lucy O'Neil. One night, after Scripps and his old woman had been out drinking on the railroad line for three or four days, he lost his wife. He didn't know where she was. When he came to himself everything was dark. He walked along the railroad track toward town. The ties were stiff and hard under his feet. He tried walking on the rails. He couldn't do it. He had the dope on that all right. He went back to walking along the ties. It was a long way into town. Finally he came to where he could see the lights of the switch-yard. He cut away from the tracks and passed the Mancelona High School. It was a yellow-brick building. There was nothing rococo about it, like the buildings he had seen in Paris. No, he had never been in Paris. That was not he. That was his friend Yogi Johnson.

Yogi Johnson looked out of the window. Soon it would be time to shut the pump-factory for the night. He opened the window carefully, just a crack. Just a crack, but that was enough. Outside in the yard the snow had begun to melt. A warm breeze was blowing. A chinook wind the pump fellows called it. The warm chinook wind came in through the window into the pump-factory. All the workmen laid down their tools. Many of them were Indians.

The foreman was a short, iron-jawed man. He had once made a trip as far as Duluth. Duluth was far across the blue waters of the lake in the hills of Minnesota. A wonderful thing had happened to him there.

The foreman put his finger in his mouth to moisten it and held it up in the air. He felt the warm breeze on his finger. He shook his head ruefully and smiled at the men, a little grimly perhaps.

'Well, it's a regular chinook, boys,' he said.

Silently for the most part, the workmen hung up their tools. The half-completed pumps were put away in their racks. The workmen filed, some of them talking, others silent, a few muttering, to the washroom to wash up.

Outside through the window came the sound of an Indian war-whoop.

Chapter 2

Scripps O'Neil stood outside the Mancelona High School looking up at the lighted windows. It was dark and the snow was falling. It had been falling ever since Scripps could remember. A passer-by stopped and stared at Scripps. After all, what was this man to him? He went on.

Scripps stood in the snow and stared up at the lighted windows of the High School. Inside there people were learning things. Far into the night they worked, the boys vying with the girls in their search for knowledge, this urge for the learning of things that was sweeping America. His girl, little Lousy, a girl that had cost him a cool seventy-five dollars in doctors' bills, was in there learning. Scripps was proud. It was too late for him to learn, but there, day after day and night after night, Lousy was learning. She had the stuff in her, that girl.

Scripps went up to his house. It was not a big house, but it wasn't the size that mattered to Scripps's old woman.

'Scripps,' she often said when they were drinking

together, 'I don't want a palace. All I want is a place to keep the wind out.' Scripps had taken her at her word. Now, as he walked in the late evening through the snow and saw the lights of his own home, he felt glad that he had taken her at her word. It was better this way than if he were coming home to a palace. He, Scripps, was not the sort of chap that wanted a palace.

He opened the door of his house and went in. Something kept going through his head. He tried to get it out, but it was no good. What was it that poet chap his friend Harry Parker had met once in Detroit had written? Harry used to recite it: 'Through pleasures and palaces though I may roam. When you something something something there's no place like home.' He could not remember the words. Not all of them. He had written a simple tune to it and taught Lucy to sing it. That was when they first were married. Scripps might have been a composer, one of these chaps that write the stuff the Chicago Symphony Orchestra plays, if he had had a chance to go on. He would get Lucy to sing that song tonight. He would never drink again. Drinking robbed him of his ear for music. Times when he was drunk the sound of the whistles of the trains at night pulling up the Boyne Falls grade seemed more lovely than anything this chap Stravinsky had ever written. Drinking had done that. It was wrong. He would get away to Paris. Like this chap Albert Spalding that played the violin.

Scripps opened the door. He went in. 'Lucy,' he called, 'it is I, Scripps.' He would never drink again. No more nights out on the railroad. Perhaps Lucy needed a new fur coat. Perhaps, after all, she had wanted a palace instead of this place. You never knew how you were treating a woman. Perhaps, after all, this place was not keeping out the wind. Fantastic. He lit a match. 'Lucy!' he called out, and there was a note of dumb terror in his mouth. His friend Walt Simmons had heard just such a cry from a stallion that had once been run over by a passing autobus in the Place Vendôme in Paris. In Paris there were no geldings. All the horses were stallions. They did not breed mares. Not since the war. The war had changed all that.

'Lucy!' he called, and again 'Lucy!' There was no answer. The house was empty. Through the snow-filled air, as he stood there alone in his tall leanness, in his own deserted house, there came to Scripps's ears the distant sound of an Indian war-whoop.

Chapter 3

Scripps left Mancelona. He was through with that place. What had a town like that to give him? There was nothing to it. You worked all your life and then a thing like that happened. The savings of years wiped out. Everything gone. He started to Chicago to get a job. Chicago was the place. Look at its geographical situation, right at the end of Lake Michigan. Chicago would do big things. Any fool could see that. He would buy land in what is now the Loop, the big shopping and manufacturing district. He would buy the land at a low price and then hang onto it. Let them try and get it away from him. He knew a thing or two now.

Alone, bareheaded, the snow blowing in his hair, he walked down the G.R.&I. railway tracks. It was the coldest night he had ever known. He picked up a dead bird that had frozen and fallen onto the railroad tracks and put it inside his shirt to warm it. The bird nestled close to his warm body and pecked at his chest gratefully.

'Poor little chap,' Scripps said. 'You feel the cold too.'

9

Tears came into his eyes.

'Drat that wind,' Scripps said and once again faced into the blowing snow. The wind was blowing straight down from Lake Superior. The telegraph wires above Scripps's head sang in the wind. Through the dark, Scripps saw a great yellow eye coming toward him. The giant locomotive came nearer through the snowstorm. Scripps stepped to one side of the track to let it go by. What is it that old writing fellow Shakespeare says: 'Might makes right'? Scripps thought of that quotation as the train went past him in the snowing darkness. First the engine passed. He saw the fireman bending to fling great shovelfuls of coal into the open furnace door. The engineer wore goggles. His face was lit up by the light from the open door of the engine. He was the engineer. It was he who had his hand on the throttle. Scripps thought of the Chicago anarchists who, when they were hanged, said: 'Though you throttle us today, still you cannot something something our souls.' There was a monument where they were buried in Waldheim Cemetery, right beside the Forest Park Amusement Park, in Chicago. His father used to take Scripps out there on Sundays. The monument was all black and there was a black angel. That was when Scripps had been a little boy. He used often to ask his father: 'Father, why if we come to look at the anarchists on Sunday why can't we ride on the shoot the chutes?' He had never been satisfied with his father's answer. He had been a little boy in knee pants then. His father had been a great composer. His mother was an Italian woman from the north of Italy.

10

They were strange people, these north Italians.

Scripps stood beside the track, and the long black segments of the train clicked by him in the snow. All the cars were Pullmans. The blinds were down. Light came in dim slits from the bottom of the dark windows as the cars went by. The train did not roar by as it might have if it had been going in the other direction, because it was climbing the Boyne Falls grade. It went slower than if it had been going down. Still it went too fast for Scripps to hitch on. He thought how he had been an expert at hitching on grocery wagons when he was a young boy in knee pants.

The long black train of Pullman cars passed Scripps as he stood beside the tracks. Who were in those cars? Were they Americans, piling up money while they slept? Were they mothers? Were they fathers? Were there lovers among them? Or were they Europeans, members of a worn-out civilization world-weary from the war? Scripps wondered.

The last car passed him and the train went on up the track. Scripps watched the red light at its stern disappearing into the blackness through which the snowflakes now came softly. The bird fluttered inside his shirt. Scripps started along the ties. He wanted to get to Chicago that night, if possible, to start work in the morning. The bird fluttered again. It was not so feeble now. Scripps put his hand on it to still its little bird flutterings. The bird was calmed. Scripps strode on up the track.

After all, he did not need to go as far as Chicago. There were other places. What if that critic fellow

Henry Mencken had called Chicago the Literary Capital of America? There was Grand Rapids. Once in Grand Rapids, he could start in the furniture business. Fortunes had been made that way. Grand Rapids furniture was famous wherever young couples walked in the evening to talk of home-making. He remembered a sign he had seen in Chicago as a little boy. His mother had pointed it out to him as together they walked barefoot through what now is probably the Loop, begging from door to door. His mother loved the bright flashing of the electric lights in the sign.

'They are like San Miniato in my native Florence,' she told Scripps. 'Look at them, my son,' she said, 'for some day your music will be played there by the Florence Symphony Orchestra.'

Scripps had often watched the sign for hours while his mother slept wrapped in an old shawl on what is now probably the Blackstone Hotel. The sign had made a great impression on him.

LET HARTMAN FEATHER YOUR NEST

it had said. It flashed in many different colours. First a pure, dazzling white. That was what Scripps loved best. Then it flashed a lovely green. Then it flashed red. One night as he lay crouched against his mother's body warmth and watched the sign flash, a policeman came up. 'You'll have to move along,' he said.

Ah, yes, there was big money to be made in the furniture business if you knew how to go about it. He,

Scripps, knew all the wrinkles of that game. In his own mind it was settled. He would stop at Grand Rapids. The little bird fluttered, happily now.

'Ah, what a beautiful gilded cage I'll build for you, my pretty one,' Scripps said exultantly. The little bird pecked him confidently. Scripps strode on in the storm. The snow was beginning to drift across the track. Borne on the wind, there came to Scripps's ears the sound of a far-off Indian war-whoop.

Chapter 4

Where was Scripps now? Walking in the night in the storm he had become confused. He had started for Chicago after that dreadful night when he had found that his home was a home no longer. Why had Lucy left? What had become of Lousy? He, Scripps, did not know. Not that he cared. That was all behind him. There was none of that now. He was standing knee-deep in snow in front of a railway station. On the railway station was written in big letters:

PETOSKEY

There were a pile of deer shipped down by hunters from the Upper Peninsula of Michigan, lying piled the one on the other, dead and stiff and drifted half over with snow on the station platform. Scripps read the sign again. Could this be Petoskey?

A man was inside the station, tapping something back of a wicketed window. He looked out at Scripps. Could he be a telegrapher? Something told Scripps that he was.

14

He stepped out of the snow-drift and approached the window. Behind the window the man worked busily away at his telegrapher's key.

'Are you a telegrapher?' asked Scripps.

'Yes sir,' said the man. 'I'm a telegrapher.'

'How wonderful.'

The telegrapher eyed him suspiciously. After all, what was this man to him?

'Is it hard to be a telegrapher?' Scripps asked. He wanted to ask the man outright if this was Petoskey. He did not know this great northern section of America, though, and he wished to be polite.

The telegrapher looked at him curiously.

'Say,' he asked, 'are you a fairy?'

'No,' Scripps said. 'I don't know what being a fairy means.'

'Well,' said the telegrapher, 'what do you carry a bird around for?'

'Bird?' asked Scripps. 'What bird?'

'That bird that's sticking out of your shirt.' Scripps was at a loss. What sort of chap was this telegrapher? What sort of men went in for telegraphy? Were they like composers? Were they like artists? Were they like writers? Were they like the advertising men who write the ads in our national weeklies? Or were they like Europeans, drawn and wasted by the war, their best years behind them? Could he tell this telegrapher the whole story? Would he understand?

'I started home,' he began. 'I passed the Mancelona High School –'

'I knew a girl in Mancelona,' the telegrapher said. 'Maybe you knew her. Ethel Enright.'

It was no good going on. He would cut the story short. He would give the bare essentials. Besides, it was beastly cold. It was cold for standing there on the wind-swept station platform. Something told him it was useless to go on. He looked over at the deer lying there in a pile, stiff and cold. Perhaps they, too, had been lovers. Some were bucks and some were does. The bucks had horns. That was how you could tell. With cats it was more difficult. In France they geld cats and do not geld the horses. France was a long way off.

'My wife left me,' Scripps said abruptly.

'I don't wonder if you go around with a damn bird sticking out of your shirt,' the telegrapher said.

'What town is this?' Scripps asked. The single moment of spiritual communion they had had, had been dissipated. They had never really had it. But they might have. It was no use now. It was no use trying to capture what was gone. What had fled.

'Petoskey,' the telegrapher replied.

'Thank you,' Scripps said. He turned and walked into the silent, deserted Northern town. Luckily, he had four hundred and fifty dollars in his pocket. He had sold a story to George Horace Lorimer just before he had started out with his old woman on that drinking trip. Why had he gone at all? What was it all about, anyway?

Coming towards him down the street came two Indians. They looked at him, but their faces did not change. Their faces remained the same. They went into McCarthy's barber shop.

16

Chapter 5

Scripps O'Neil stood irresolutely before the barber shop. Inside there men were being shaved. Other men, no different, were having their hair cut. Other men sat against the wall in tall chairs and smoked, awaiting their turn in the barber chairs, admiring the paintings hung on the wall, or admiring their own reflections in the long mirror. Should he, Scripps, go in there? After all, he had four hundred and fifty dollars in his pocket. He could go where he wanted. He looked, once again, irresolutely. It was an inviting prospect, the society of men, the warm room, the white jackets of the barbers skillfully snipping away with their scissors or drawing their blades diagonally through the lather that covered the face of some man who was getting a shave. They could use their tools, these barbers. Somehow, it wasn't what he wanted. He wanted something different. He wanted to eat. Besides, there was his bird to look after.

Scripps O'Neil turned his back on the barber shop and strode away up the street of the silently frozen Northern town. On his right, as he walked, the weeping birches, their branches bare of leaves, hung down to the ground, heavy with snow. To his ears came the sound of sleigh bells. Perhaps it was Christmas. In the South little children would be shooting off firecrackers and crying 'Christmas Gift! Christmas Gift!' to one another. His father came from the South. He had been a soldier in the rebel army. 'Way back in Civil War days. Sherman had burned their house down on his March to the Sea. 'War is hell,' Sherman had said. 'But you see how it is, Mrs O'Neil. I've got to do it.' He had touched a match to the white-pillared old house.

'If General O'Neil were here, you dastard!' his mother had said, speaking in her broken English, 'you'd never have touched a match to that house.'

Smoke curled up from the old house. The fire was mounting. The white pillars were obscured in the rising smoke-wreaths. Scripps had held close to his mother's linsey-woolsey dress.

General Sherman climbed back onto his horse and made a low bow. 'Mrs O'Neil,' he said, and Scripps's mother always said there were tears in his eyes, even if he was a damned Yank. The man had a heart, sir, even if he did not follow its dictates. 'Mrs O'Neil, if the general were here, we could have it out as man to man. As it is, ma'am, war being what it is, I must burn your house.'

He motioned to one of his soldiers, who ran forward and threw a bucket of kerosene on the flames. The flames rose and a great column of smoke went up in the still evening air.

'At least, General Sherman,' Scripps's mother said triumphantly, 'that column of smoke will warn the other loyal daughters of the Confederacy that you are coming.'

Sherman bowed. 'That is a risk we must take, ma'am.' He clapped spurs to his horse and rode away. His long white hair floating in the wind. Neither Scripps nor his mother ever saw him again. Odd that he should think of that incident now. He looked up. Facing him was a sign:

BROWN'S BEANERY THE BEST BY TEST

He would go in and eat. This was what he wanted. He would go in and eat. That sign:

THE BEST BY TEST

Ah, these big beanery owners were wise fellows. They knew how to get the customers. No ads in *The Saturday Evening Post* for them. THE BEST BY TEST. That was the stuff. He went in.

Inside the door of the beanery Scripps O'Neil looked around him. There was a long counter. There was a clock. There was a door let into the kitchen. There were a couple of tables. There were a pile of doughnuts under a glass cover. There were signs put about on the wall advertising things one might eat. Was this, after all, Brown's Beanery?

'I wonder,' Scripps asked an elderly waitress who

19

came in through the swing door from the kitchen, 'if you could tell me if this is Brown's Beanery?'

'Yes sir,' answered the waitress. 'The best by test.'

'Thank you,' Scripps said. He sat down at the counter. 'I would like to have some beans for myself and some for my bird here.'

He opened his shirt and placed the bird on the counter. The bird ruffled his feathers and shook himself. He pecked inquiringly at the catsup bottle. The elderly waitress put out a hand and stroked him. 'Isn't he a manly little fellow?' she remarked. 'By the way,' she asked, a little shamefacedly, 'what was it you ordered, sir?'

'Beans,' Scripps said, 'for my bird and myself.'

The waitress shoved up a little wicket that led into the kitchen. Scripps had a glimpse of a warm, steam-filled room, with big pots and kettles, and many shining cans on the wall.

'A pig and the noisy ones,' the waitress called in a matter-of-fact voice into the open wicket. 'One for a bird!'

'On the fire!' a voice answered from the kitchen.

'How old is your bird?' the elderly waitress asked.

'I don't know,' Scripps said. 'I never saw him before last night. I was walking on the railroad track from Mancelona. My wife left me.'

'Poor little chap,' the waitress said. She poured a little catsup on her finger and the bird pecked at it gratefully.

'My wife left me,' Scripps said. 'We'd been out drinking on the railroad track. We used to go out

20

evenings and watch the trains pass. I write stories. I had a story in *The Post* and two in *The Dial*. Mencken's trying to get ahold of me. I'm too wise for that sort of thing. No politzei for mine. They give me the katzenjammers.'

What was he saying? He was talking wildly. This would never do. He must pull himself together.

'Schofield Thayer was my best man,' he said. 'I'm a Harvard man. All I want is for them to give me and my bird a square deal. No more *weltpolitik*. Take Dr Coolidge away.'

His mind was wandering. He knew what it was. He was faint with hunger. This Northern air was too sharp, too keen for him.

'I say,' he said. 'Could you let me have just a few of those beans. I don't like to rush things. I know when to let well enough alone.'

The wicket came up, and a large plate of beans and a small plate of beans, both steaming, appeared.

'Here they are,' the waitress said.

Scripps fell to on the large plate of beans. There was a little pork, too. The bird was eating happily, raising its head after each swallow to let the beans go down.

'He does that to thank God for those beans,' the elderly waitress explained.

'They're mighty fine beans, too,' Scripps agreed. Under the influence of the beans his head was clearing. What was this rot he had been talking about that man Henry Mencken? Was Mencken really after him? It wasn't a pretty prospect to face. He had four hundred and fifty dollars in his pocket. When that was gone he

21

could always put an end to things. If they pressed him too far they would get a big surprise. He wasn't the man to be taken alive. Just let them try it.

After eating his beans the bird had fallen asleep. He was sleeping on one leg, the other tucked up into his feathers.

'When he gets tired of sleeping on that leg he will change legs and rest,' the waitress remarked. 'We had an old osprey at home that was like that.

'Where was your home?' Scripps asked.

'In England. In the Lake District,' The waitress smiled a bit wistfully. 'Wordsworth's country, you know.'

Ah, these English. They travelled all over the face of the globe, they were not content to remain in their little island. Strange Nordics, obsessed with their dream of empire.

'I was not always a waitress,' the elderly waitress remarked.

'I'm sure you weren't.'

'Not half,' the waitress went on. 'It's rather a strange story. Perhaps it would bore you?'

'Not at all,' Scripps said. 'You wouldn't mind if I used the story sometime?'

'Not if you find it interesting,' the waitress smiled. 'You wouldn't use my name, of course.'

'Not if you'd rather not,' Scripps said. 'By the way, could I have another order of beans?'

'Best by test,' the waitress smiled. Her face was lined and grey. She looks a little like that actress that died in Pittsburgh. What was her name? Lenore Ulric. In *Peter*

22

Pan. That was it. They say she always went about veiled, Scripps thought. There was an interesting woman. Was it Lenore Ulric? Perhaps not. No matter.

'You really want some more beans?' asked the waitress.

'Yes,' Scripps answered simply.

'Once again on the loud ones,' the waitress called into the wicket. 'Lay off the bird.'

'On the fire,' came the response.

'Please go on with your story,' Scripps said kindly.

'It was the year of the Paris Exposition,' she began. 'I was a young girl at the time, a *jeune fille,* and I came over from England with my mother. We were going to be present at the opening of the exposition. On our way from the Gare du Nord to the hotel in the Place Vendôme where we lodged, we stopped at a coiffeur's shop and made some trifling purchase. My mother, as I recall, purchased an additional bottle of "smelling salts", as you call them here in America.'

She smiled.

'Yes, go on. Smelling salts,' Scripps said.

'We registered, as is customary, in the hotel, and were given the adjoining rooms we had reserved. My mother felt a bit done in by the trip, and we dined in our rooms. I was full of excitement about seeing the exposition on the morrow. But I was tired after the journey – we had had a rather nasty crossing – and slept soundly. In the morning I awoke and called for my mother. There was no answer, and I went into the room to waken Mummy. Instead of Mummy there was a French general in the bed.'

'Mon Dieu!' Scripps said.

'I was terribly frightened,' the waitress went on, 'and rang the bell for the management. The concierge came up, and I demanded to know where my mother was.

'"But, mademoiselle," the concierge explained, "we know nothing about your mother. You came here with General so-and-so" – I cannot remember the general's name.'

'Call him General Joffre,' Scripps suggested.

'It was a name very like that,' the waitress said. 'I was fearfully frightened and sent for the police, and demanded to see the guest-register. "You'll find there that I am registered with my mother," I said. The police came and the concierge brought up the register. "See, madame," he said. "You are registered with the general with whom you came to our hotel last night."

'I was desperate. Finally, I remembered where the coiffeur's shop was. The police sent for the coiffeur. An agent of police brought him in.

'"I stopped at your shop with my mother," I said to the coiffeur, "and my mother bought a bottle of aromatic salts."

'"I remember mademoiselle perfectly," the coiffeur said. "But you were not with your mother. You were with an elderly French general. He purchased, I believe, a pair of mustache tongs. My books, at any rate, will show the purchase."

'I was in despair. In the meantime the police had brought in the cab driver who had brought us from the gare to the hotel. He swore that I had never been with my mother. Tell me, does this story bore you?'

24

'Go on,' said Scripps. 'If you had ever been as hard up for plots as I have been!'

'Well,' the waitress said. 'That's all there is to the tale. I never saw my mother again. I communicated with the embassy, but they could do nothing. It was finally established by them that I had crossed the channel with my mother, but they could do nothing beyond that.' Tears came into the elderly waitress's eyes. 'I never saw Mummy again. Never again. Not even once.'

'What about the general?'

'He finally loaned me one hundred francs – not a great sum even in those days – and I came to America and became a waitress. That's all there is to the story.'

'There's more than that,' Scripps said. 'I'd stake my life there's more than that.'

'Sometimes, you know, I feel there is,' the waitress said. 'I feel there must be more than that. Somewhere, somehow, there must be an explanation. I don't know what brought the subject into my mind this morning.'

'It was a good thing to get it off your mind,' Scripps said.

'Yes,' the waitress smiled, the lines in her face not quite so deep now. 'I feel better now.'

'Tell me,' Scripps asked the waitress. 'Is there any work in this town for me and my bird?'

'Honest work?' asked the waitress. 'I only know of honest work.'

'Yes, honest work,' Scripps said.

'They do say they're hiring hands at the new pump-factory,' the waitress said. Why shouldn't he work with

25

his hands? Rodin had done it. Cézanne had been a butcher. Renoir a carpenter. Picasso had worked in a cigarette-factory in his boyhood. Gilbert Stuart, who painted those famous portraits of Washington that are reproduced all over this America of ours and hang in every schoolroom – Gilbert Stuart had been a blacksmith. Then there was Emerson. Emerson had been a hod-carrier. James Russell Lowell had been, he had heard, a telegraph operator in his youth. Like that chap down in the station. Perhaps even now that telegrapher at the station was working on his 'Thanatopsis' or his 'To a Waterfowl' Why shouldn't he, Scripps O'Neil, work in a pump-factory?

'You'll come back again?' the waitress asked.

'If I may,' Scripps said.

'And bring your bird.'

'Yes,' Scripps said. 'The little chap's rather tired now. After all, it was a hard night for him.'

'I should say it was,' agreed the waitress.

Scripps went out again into the town. He felt clear-headed and ready to face life. A pump-factory would be interesting. Pumps were big things now. Fortunes were made and lost in pumps every day in New York in Wall Street. He knew of a chap who'd cleaned up a cool half-million on pumps in less than half an hour. They knew what they were about, these big Wall Street operators.

Outside on the street he looked up at the sign. BEST BY TEST, he read. They had the dope all right, he said. Was it true, though, that there had been a Negro cook? Just once, just for a moment, when the

26

wicket went up, he thought he had caught a glimpse of something black. Perhaps the chap was only sooty from the stove.

PART TWO

The Struggle for Life

And here I solemnly protest I have no intention to vilify or asperse any one; for though everything is copied from the book of nature, and scarce a character or action produced which I have not taken from my own observations or experience; yet I have used the utmost care to obscure the persons by such different circumstances, degrees, and colors, that it will be impossible to guess at them with any degree of certainty; and if it ever happens otherwise, it is only where the failure characterized is so minute, that it is a foible only which the party himself may laugh at as well as any other.

HENRY FIELDING

Chapter 6

Scripps O'Neil was looking for employment. It would
be good to work with his hands. He walked down the
street away from the beanery and past McCarthy's
barber shop. He did not go into the barber shop. It
looked as inviting as ever, but it was employment
Scripps wanted. He turned sharply around the corner
of the barber shop and onto the Main Street of
Petoskey. It was a handsome, broad street, lined on
either side with brick and pressed-stone buildings.
Scripps walked along it toward the part of town where
the pump-factory stood. At the door of the pump-
factory he was embarrassed. Could this really be the
pump-factory? True, a stream of pumps were being
carried out and set up in the snow, and workmen were
throwing pails of water over them to encase them in a
coating of ice that would protect them from the winter
winds as well as any paint would. But were they really
pumps? It might be a trick. The pump men were clever
fellows.

'I say!' Scripps beckoned to one of the workmen
who was sloshing water over a new, raw-looking pump

that had just been carried out and stood protestingly in the snow. 'Are they pumps?'

'They will be in time,' the workman said.

Scripps knew it was the factory. They weren't going to fool him on that. He walked up to the door. There was a sign on it:

KEEP OUT. THIS MEANS YOU

Can that mean me? Scripps wondered. He knocked on the door and went in.

'I'd like to speak to the manager,' he said standing quietly in the half-light.

Workmen were passing him, carrying the new raw pumps on their shoulders. They hummed snatches of songs as they passed. The handles of the pumps flopped stiffly in dumb protest. Some pumps had no handles. They perhaps, after all, are the lucky ones, Scripps thought. A little man came up to him. He was well-built, short, with wide shoulders and a grim face.

'You were asking for the manager?'

'Yes, sir.'

'I'm the foreman here. What I say goes.'

'Can you hire and fire?' Scripps asked.

'I can do one as easily as the other,' the foreman said.

'I want a job.'

'Any experience?'

'Not in pumps.'

'All right,' the foreman said. 'We'll put you on piecework. Here, Yogi,' he called to one of the men, who was standing looking out of the window of the factory, 'show this new chum where to stow his swag and how to find his way around these diggings.' The foreman looked Scripps up and down. 'I'm an Australian,' he said. 'Hope you'll like the lay here.' He walked off.

The man called Yogi Johnson came over from the window. 'Glad to meet you,' he said. He was a chunky, well-built fellow. One of the sort you see around almost anywhere. He looked as though he had been through things.

'Your foreman's the first Australian I've ever met,' Scripps said.

'Oh, he's not Australian,' Yogi said. 'He was just with the Australians once during the war, and it made a big impression on him.'

'Were you in the war?' Scripps asked.

'Yes,' Yogi Johnson said. 'I was the first man to go from Cadillac.'

'It must have been quite an experience.'

'It meant a lot to me,' Yogi answered. 'Come on and I'll show you around the works.'

Scripps followed this man, who showed him through the pump-factory. It was dark but warm inside the pump-factory. Men naked to the waist took the pumps in huge tongs as they came trundling by on an endless chain, culling out the misfits and placing the perfect pumps on another endless chain that carried them up to the cooling room. Other men, Indians for the most part, wearing only breech-clouts, broke up the misfit pumps with huge hammers and adzes and rapidly recast them into axe heads, wagon springs,

33

trombone slides, bullet moulds, all the by-products of a big pump-factory. There was nothing wasted. Yogi pointed out. A group of Indian boys were humming to themselves one of the old tribal chanties, squatted in a corner of the big forging room shaping the little fragments that were chipped from the pumps in casting, into safety razor blades.

'They work naked,' Yogi said. 'They're searched as they go out. Sometimes they try and conceal the razor blades and take them out with them to bootleg.'

'There must be quite a loss that way,' Scripps said.

'Oh, no,' Yogi answered. 'The inspectors get most of them.'

Upstairs, apart in a separate room, two old men were working. Yogi opened the door. One of the old men looked over his steel spectacles and frowned.

'You make a draft,' he said.

'Shut the door,' the other old man said, in the high, complaining voice of the very old.

'They're our two hand-workers,' Yogi said. 'They make all the pumps the manufactory sends out to the big international pump races. You remember our Peerless Pounder that won the pump race in Italy, where Franky Dawson was killed?'

'I read about it in the paper,' Scripps answered.

'Mr Borrow, over there in the corner, made the Peerless Pounder all himself by hand,' Yogi said.

'I carved it direct from the steel with this knife.' Mr Borrow held up a short-bladed, razorlike-looking knife. 'Took me eighteen months to get it right.'

'The Peerless Pounder was quite a pump all right,'

34

the high-voiced little man said. 'But we're working on one now that will show its heels to any of them foreign pumps, aren't we, Henry?'

'That's Mr Shaw,' Yogi said in an undertone. 'He's probably the greatest living pump-maker.'

'You boys get along and leave us alone,' Mr Borrow said. He was carving away steadily, his infirm old hands shaking a little between strokes.

'Let the boys watch,' Mr Shaw said. 'Where you from, young feller?'

'I've just come from Mancelona,' Scripps answered. 'My wife left me.'

'Well, you won't have no difficulty finding another one,' Mr Shaw said. 'You're a likely-looking young feller. But take my advice and take your time. A poor wife ain't much better than no wife at all.'

'I wouldn't say that, Henry,' Mr Borrow remarked in his high voice. 'Any wife at all's a pretty good wife the way things are going now.'

'You take my advice, young feller, and go slow. Get yourself a good one this time.'

'Henry knows a thing or two,' Mr Borrow said. 'He knows what he's talking about there.' He laughed a high, cackling laugh. Mr Shaw, the old pump-maker, blushed.

'You boys get along and leave us get on with our pump-making,' he said. 'Henry and me here, we got a sight of work to do.'

'I'm very glad to have met you,' Scripps said.

'Come on,' Yogi said. 'I better get you started or the foreman will be on my tail.'

He put Scripps to work collaring pistons in the piston-collaring room. There Scripps worked for almost a year. In some ways it was the happiest year of his life. In other ways it was a nightmare. A hideous nightmare. In the end he grew to like it. In other ways he hated it. Before he knew it, a year had passed. He was still collaring pistons. But what strange things had happened in that year. Often he wondered about them. As he wondered, collaring a piston now almost automatically, he listened to the laughter that came up from below, where the little Indian lads were shaping what were to be razor blades. As he listened something rose in his throat and almost choked him.

Chapter 7

That night, after his first day in the pump-factory, the first day in what was or were to become an endless succession of days of dull piston-collaring, Scripps went again to the beanery to eat. All day he had kept his bird concealed. Something told him that the pump-factory was not the place to bring his bird out in. During the day the bird had several times made him uncomfortable, but he had adjusted his clothes to it and even cut a little slit the bird could poke his beak out through in search of fresh air. Now the day's work was over. It was finished. Scripps on his way to the beanery. Scripps happy that he was working with his hands. Scripps thinking of the old pump-makers. Scripps going to the society of the friendly waitress. Who was that waitress, anyway? What was it had happened to her in Paris? He must find out more about this Paris. Yogi Johnson had been there. He would quiz Yogi. Get him to talk. Draw him out. Make him tell what he knew. He knew a trick or two about that.

Watching the sunset out over the Petoskey Harbor, the lake now frozen and great blocks of ice jutting up over the breakwater, Scripps strode down the street of Petoskey to the beanery. He would have liked to ask Yogi Johnson to eat with him, but he didn't dare. Not yet. That would come later. All in good time. No need to rush matters with a man like Yogi. Who was Yogi, anyway? Had he really been in the war? What had the war meant to him? Was he really the first man to enlist from Cadillac? Where was Cadillac, anyway? Time would tell.

Scripps O'Neil opened the door and went into the beanery. The elderly waitress got up from the chair where she had been reading the overseas edition of *The Manchester Guardian*, and put the paper and her steel-rimmed spectacles on top of the cash register.

'Good evening,' she said simply. 'It's good to have *you* back.'

Something stirred inside Scripps O'Neil. A feeling that he could not define came within him.

'I've been working all day long' – he looked at the elderly waitress – 'for *you*,' he added.

'How lovely!' she said. And then smiled shyly. 'And I have been working all day long – for *you*.'

Tears came into Scripps's eyes. Something stirred inside him again. He reached forward to take the elderly waitress's hand, and with quiet dignity she laid it within his own. 'You are my woman,' he said. Tears came into her eyes, too.

'You are my man,' she said.

'Once again I say: you are my woman.' Scripps pronounced the words solemnly. Something had broken inside him again. He felt he could not keep from crying.

38

'Let this be our wedding ceremony,' the elderly waitress said. Scripps pressed her hand. 'You are my woman,' he said simply.

'You are my man and more than my man.' She looked into his eyes. 'You are all of America to me.'

'Let us go,' Scripps said.

'Have you your bird?' asked the waitress, laying aside her apron and folding the copy of *The Manchester Guardian Weekly*. 'I'll bring *The Guardian*, if you don't mind,' she said, wrapping the paper in her apron. 'It's a new paper and I've not read it yet.'

'I'm very fond of *The Guardian*,' Scripps said. 'My family have taken it ever since I can remember. My father was a great admirer of Gladstone.'

'My father went to Eton with Gladstone,' the elderly waitress said. 'And now I am ready.'

She had donned a coat and stood ready, her apron, her steel-rimmed spectacles in their worn black morocco case, her copy of *The Manchester Guardian* held in her hand.

'Have you no hat?' asked Scripps.

'No.'

'Then I will buy you one,' Scripps said tenderly.

'It will be your wedding gift,' the elderly waitress said. Again tears shone in her eyes.

'And now let us go,' Scripps said.

The elderly waitress came out from behind the counter, and together, hand in hand, they strode out into the night.

Inside the beanery the black cook pushed up the wicket and looked through from the kitchen. 'Dey've gone off,' he chuckled. 'Gone off into de night. Well, well, well,' He closed the wicket softly. Even he was a little impressed.

Chapter 8

Half an hour later Scripps O'Neil and the elderly waitress returned to the beanery as man and wife. The beanery looked much the same. There was the long counter, the salt cellars, the sugar containers, the catsup bottle, the Worcestershire Sauce bottle. There was the wicket that led into the kitchen. Behind the counter was the relief waitress. She was a buxom, jolly-looking girl, and she wore a white apron. At the counter, reading a Detroit paper, sat a drummer. The drummer was eating a T-bone steak and hashed-brown potatoes. Something very beautiful had happened to Scripps and the elderly waitress. Now they were hungry. They wished to eat.

The elderly waitress looking at Scripps. Scripps looking at the elderly waitress. The drummer reading his paper and occasionally putting a little catsup on his hashed-brown potatoes. The other waitress, Mandy, back of the counter in her freshly starched white apron. The frost on the windows. The warmth inside. The cold outside. Scripps's bird, rather rumpled now, sitting on the counter and preening his feathers.

'So you've come back,' Mandy the waitress said. 'The cook said you had gone out into the night.'

The elderly waitress looked at Mandy, her eyes brightened, her voice calm and now of a deeper, richer timbre.

'We are man and wife now,' she said kindly. 'We have just been married. What would you like to eat for supper, Scripps, dear?'

'I don't know,' Scripps said. He felt vaguely uneasy. Something was stirring within him.

'Perhaps you have eaten enough of the beans, dear Scripps,' the elderly waitress, now his wife, said. The drummer looked up from his paper. Scripps noticed that it was the Detroit *News*. There was a fine paper.

'That's a fine paper you're reading,' Scripps said to the drummer.

'It's a good paper, the *News*,' the drummer said. 'You two on your honeymoon?'

'Yes,' Mrs Scripps said; 'we are man and wife now.'

'Well,' said the drummer, 'that's a mighty fine thing to be. I'm a married man myself.'

'Are you?' said Scripps. 'My wife left me. It was in Mancelona.'

'Don't let's talk of that any more, Scripps, dear,' Mrs Scripps said. 'You've told that story so many times.'

'Yes, dear,' Scripps agreed. He felt vaguely mistrustful of himself. Something, somewhere was stirring inside of him. He looked at the waitress called Mandy, standing robust and lovely in her newly starched white apron. He watched her hands, healthy, calm, capable hands, doing the duties of her waitresshood.

'Try one of these T-bones with hashed-brown potatoes,' the drummer suggested. 'They got a nice T-bone here.'

'Would you like one, dear?' Scripps asked his wife.

'I'll just have a bowl of milk and crackers,' the elderly Mrs Scripps said. 'You have whatever you want, dear.'

'Here's your crackers and milk, Diana,' Mandy said, placing them on the counter. 'Do you want a T-bone sir?'

'Yes,' Scripps said. Something stirred again within him.

'Well done or rare?'

'Rare, please.'

The waitress turned and called into the wicket: 'Tea for one. Let it go raw!'

'Thank you,' Scripps said. He eyed the waitress Mandy. She had a gift for the picturesque in speech, that girl. It had been that very picturesque quality in her speech that had first drawn him to his present wife. That and her strange background. England, the Lake Country. Scripps striding through the Lake Country with Wordsworth. A field of golden daffodils. The wind blowing at Windermere. Far off, perhaps, a stag at bay. Ah that was farther north, in Scotland. They were a hardy race, those Scots, deep in their mountain fastnesses. Harry Lauder and his pipe. The High-landers in the Great War. Why had not he, Scripps, been in the war? That was where that chap Yogi Johnson had it on him. The war would have meant much to him, Scripps. Why hadn't he been in it? Why hadn't he heard of it in time? Perhaps he was too old.

Look at that old French General Joffre, though. Surely he was a younger man than that old general. General Foch praying for victory. The French troops kneeling along the Chemin des Dames, praying for victory. The Germans with their '*Gott mit uns.*' What a mockery. Surely he was no older than that French General Foch. He wondered.

Mandy, the waitress placed his T-bone steak and hashed-brown potatoes on the counter before him. As she laid the plate down, just for an instant, her hand touched his. Scripps felt a strange thrill go through him. Life was before him. He was not an old man. Why were there no wars now? Perhaps there were. Men were fighting in China, Chinamen, Chinamen killing one another. What for? Scripps wondered. What was it all about, anyway?

Mandy, the buxom waitress, leaned forward. 'Say,' she said, 'did I ever tell you about the last words of Henry James?'

'Really, dear Mandy,' Mrs Scripps said, 'you've told that story rather often.'

'Let's hear it,' Scripps said. 'I'm very interested in Henry James.' Henry James, Henry James. That chap who had gone away from his own land to live in England among Englishmen. Why had he done it? For what had he left America? Weren't his roots here? His brother William. Boston. Pragmatism. Harvard University. Old John Harvard with silver buckles on his shoes. Charley Brickley. Eddie Mahan. Where were they now?

'Well,' Mandy began, 'Henry James became a

British subject on his death-bed. At once, as soon as the king heard Henry James had become a British subject he sent around the highest decoration in his power to bestow – the Order of Merit.'

'The O.M.,' the elderly Mrs Scripps explained.

'That was it,' the waitress said. 'Professors Gosse and Saintsbury came with the man who brought the decoration. Henry James was lying on his death-bed, and his eyes were shut. There was a single candle on a table beside the bed. The nurse allowed them to come near the bed, and they put the ribbon of the decoration around James's neck, and the decoration lay on the sheet over Henry James's chest. Professors Gosse and Saintsbury leaned forward and smoothed the ribbon of the decoration. Henry James never opened his eyes. The nurse told them they all must go out of the room, and they all went out of the room. When they were all gone, Henry James spoke to the nurse. He never opened his eyes. 'Nurse,' Henry James said, 'put out the candle, nurse, and spare my blushes.' Those were the last words he ever spoke.'

'James was quite a writer,' Scripps O'Neil said. He was strangely moved by the story.

'You don't always tell it the same way, dear,' Mrs Scripps remarked to Mandy. There were tears in Mandy's eyes. 'I feel very strongly about Henry James,' she said.

'What was the matter with James?' asked the drummer. 'Wasn't America good enough for him?'

Scripps O'Neil was thinking about Mandy, the waitress. What a background she must have, that girl!

What a fund of anecdotes! A chap could go far with a woman like that to help him! He stroked the little bird that sat on the lunch-counter before him. The bird pecked at his finger. Was the little bird a hawk? A falcon, perhaps, from one of the big Michigan falconries. Was it perhaps a robin? Pulling and tugging at the early worm on some green lawn somewhere? He wondered.

'What do you call your bird?' the drummer asked.

'I haven't named him yet. What would you call him?'

'Why not call him Ariel?' Mandy asked.

'Or Puck,' Mrs Scripps put in.

'What's it mean?' asked the drummer.

'It's a character out of Shakespeare,' Mandy explained.

'Oh, give the bird a chance.'

'What would you call him?' Scripps turned to the drummer.

'He ain't a parrot, is he?' asked the drummer. 'If he was a parrot you could call him Polly.'

'There's a character in "The Beggar's Opera" called Polly,' Mandy explained.

Scripps wondered. Perhaps the bird was a parrot. A parrot strayed from some comfortable home with some old maid. The untilled soil of some New England spinster.

'Better wait till you see how he turns out,' the drummer advised. 'You got plenty of time to name him.'

This drummer had sound ideas. He, Scripps, did not

46

even know what sex the bird was. Whether he was a boy bird or a girl bird.

'Wait till you see if he lays eggs,' the drummer suggested. Scripps looked into the drummer's eyes. The fellow had voiced his own unspoken thought.

'You know a thing or two, drummer,' he said.

'Well,' the drummer admitted modestly, 'I ain't drummed all these years for nothing.'

'You're right there, pal,' Scripps said.

'That's a nice bird you got there, brother,' the drummer said. 'You want to hang onto that bird.'

Scripps knew it. Ah, these drummers know a thing or two. Going up and down over the face of this great America of ours. These drummers kept their eyes open. They were no fools.

'Listen,' the drummer said. He pushed his derby hat off his brow and, leaning forward, spat into a tall brass cuspidor that stood beside his stool. 'I want to tell you about a pretty beautiful thing that happened to me once in Bay City.'

Mandy, the waitress leaned forward. Mrs Scripps leaned toward the drummer to hear better. The drummer looked apologetically at Scripps and stroked the bird with his forefinger.

'Tell you about it some other time, brother,' he said. Scripps understood. From out of the kitchen, through the wicket in the hall, came a high-pitched, haunting laugh. Scripps listened. Could that be the laughter of the Negro? He wondered.

Chapter 9

Scripps going slowly to work in the pump-factory in the mornings. Mrs Scripps looking out of the window and watching him go up the street. Not much time for reading *The Guardian* now. Not much time for reading about English politics. Not much time for worrying about the cabinet crises over there in France. The French were a strange people. Joan of Arc. Eva le Gallienne. Clemenceau. Georges Carpentier. Sacha Guitry. Yvonne Printemps. Grock. Les Fratellinis. Gilbert Seldes. *The Dial*. *The Dial* Prize. Marianne Moore. E.E. Cummings. *The Enormous Room*. *Vanity Fair*. Frank Crowninshield. What was it all about? Where was it taking her?

She had a man now. A man of her own. For her own. Could she keep him? Could she hold him for her own? She wondered.

Mrs Scripps, formerly an elderly waitress, now the wife of Scripps O'Neil, with a good job in the pump-factory. Diana Scripps. Diana was her own name. It had been her mother's too. Diana Scripps looking into the mirror and wondering could she hold him. It was getting to be a question. Why had he ever met Mandy? Would she have the courage to break off going to the restaurant with Scripps to eat? She couldn't do that. He would go alone. She knew that. It was no use trying to pull wool over her own eyes. He would go alone and he would talk with Mandy. Diana looked into the mirror. Could she hold him? Could she hold him? That thought never left her now.

Every night in the restaurant, she couldn't call it a beanery now – that made a lump come in her throat and made her throat feel hard and choky. Every night at the restaurant now Scripps and Mandy talked together. The girl was trying to take him away. Him, her Scripps. Trying to take him away. Take him away. Could she, Diana, hold him?

She was no better than a slut, that Mandy. Was that the way to do? Was that the thing to do? Go after another woman's man? Come between man and wife? Break up a home? And all with these interminable literary reminiscences. These endless anecdotes. Scripps was fascinated by Mandy. Diana admitted that to herself. But she might hold him. That was all that mattered now. To hold him. To hold him. Not to let him go. Make him stay. She looked into the mirror.

Diana subscribing for *The Forum*. Diana reading *The Mentor*. Diana reading William Lyon Phelps in *Scribner's*. Diana walking through the frozen streets of the silent Northern town to the Public Library, to read *The Literary Digest* "Book Review". Diana waiting for the postman to come, bringing *The Bookman*. Diana, in the snow, waiting for the postman to bring *The*

Saturday Review of Literature. Diana, bareheaded now, standing in the mounting snowdrifts, waiting for the postman to bring her the New York *Times* "Literary Section". Was it doing any good? Was it holding him?

At first it seemed to be. Diana learned editorials by John Farrar by heart. Scripps brightened. A little of the old light shining in Scripps's eyes now. Then it died. Some little mistake in the wording, some slip in her understanding of a phrase, some divergence in her attitude made it all ring false. She would go on. She was not beaten. He was her man and she would hold him. She looked away from the window and slit open the covering of the magazine that lay on her table. It was *Harper's Magazine*. *Harper's Magazine* in a new format. *Harper's Magazine* completely changed and revised. Perhaps that would do the trick. She wondered.

Chapter 10

Spring was coming. Spring was in the air. (Author's Note. – This is the same day on which the story starts, back on page three.) A chinook wind was blowing. Workmen were coming home from the factory. Scripps's bird singing in its cage. Diana looking out of the open window. Diana watching for her Scripps to come up the street. Could she hold him? Could she hold him? If she couldn't hold him would he leave her his bird. She had felt lately that she couldn't hold him. In the nights, now, when she touched Scripps he rolled away, not toward her. It was a little sign, but life was made up of little signs. She felt she couldn't hold him. As she looked out of the window, a copy of *The Century Magazine* dropped from her nerveless hand. *The Century* had a new editor. There were more woodcuts. Glen Frank had gone to head some great university somewhere. There were more Van Dorens on the magazine. Diana felt that might turn the trick. Happily she had opened *The Century* and read all morning. Then the wind, the warm chinook wind, had started to blow, and she knew Scripps would soon be home. Men were coming down the street in increasing numbers. Was Scripps among them? She did not like to put on her spectacles to look. She wanted Scripps's first glimpse of her to be of her at her best. As she felt him drawing nearer, the confidence she had had in *The Century* grew fainter. She had so hoped that would give her something which would hold him. She wasn't sure now.

Scripps coming down the street with a crowd of excited workmen. Men stirred by the spring. Scripps swinging his lunch-bucket. Scripps waving good-by to the workmen, who trooped one by one into what had formerly been a saloon. Scripps not looking up at the window. Scripps coming up the stairs. Scripps coming nearer. Scripps coming nearer. Scripps here.

'Good afternoon, dear Scripps,' she said. 'I've been reading a story by Ruth Suckow.'

'Hello, Diana,' Scripps answered. He set down his lunch-pail. She looked worn and old. He could afford to be polite.

'What was the story about, Diana?' he asked.

'It was about a little girl in Iowa,' Diana said, she moved towards him. 'It was about people on the land. It reminded me a little of my own Lake Country.'

'That so?' asked Scripps. In some ways the pump-factory had hardened him. His speech had become more clipped. More like these hardy Northern workers'. But his mind was the same.

'Would you like me to read a little of it out loud?' Diana asked. 'They're some lovely woodcuts.'

'How about going down to the beanery?' Scripps said.

'As you wish, dear,' Diana said. Then her voice broke. 'I wish – oh, I wish you'd never seen that place!' She wiped away her tears. Scripps had not even seen them. 'I'll bring the bird, dear,' Diana said. 'He hasn't been out all day.'

Together they went down the street to the beanery. They did not walk hand in hand now. They walked like what are called old married people. Mrs Scripps carried the bird-cage. The bird was happy in the warm wind. Men lurching along, drunk with the spring, passed them. Many spoke to Scripps. He was well known and well liked in the town now. Some, as they lurched by, raised their hats to Mrs Scripps. She responded vaguely. If I can only hold him, she was thinking. If I can only hold him. As they walked along the slushy snow of the narrow sidewalk of the Northern town, something began to beat in her head. Perhaps it was the rhythm of their walking together. I can't hold him. I can't hold him. I can't hold him.

Scripps took her arm as they crossed the street. When his hand touched her arm Diana knew it was true. She would never hold him. A group of Indians passed them on the street. Were they laughing at her or was it some tribal jest? Diana didn't know. All she knew was that rhythm that beat into her brain. I can't hold him. I can't hold him.

AUTHOR'S NOTE:

For the reader, not the printer. What difference does it make to the printer? Who is the printer, anyway? Gutenberg. The Gutenberg Bible. Caxton. Twelve-point open-face Caslon. The linotype machine. The author as a little boy being sent to look for type lice. The author as a young man being sent for the key to the forms. Ah, they knew a trick or two, these printers.

(In case the reader is becoming confused, we are now up to where the story opened with Yogi Johnson and Scripps O'Neil in the pump-factory itself, with the chinook wind blowing. As you see, Scripps O'Neil had now come out of the pump-factory and is on his way to the beanery with his wife, who is afraid she cannot hold him. Personally, we don't believe she can, but the reader will see for himself. We will now leave the couple on their way to the beanery and go back and take up Yogi Johnson. We want the reader to like Yogi Johnson. The story will move a little faster from now on, in case any of the readers are tiring. We will also try and work in a number of good anecdotes. Would it be any violation of confidence if we told the reader that we get the best of these anecdotes from Mr Ford Madox Ford? We owe him our thanks, and we hope the reader does, too. At any rate, we will now go on with Yogi Johnson. Yogi Johnson, the reader may remember, is the chap who was in the war. As the story opens, he is just coming out of the pump-factory. (See page three.)

It is very hard to write this way, beginning things backward, and the author hopes the reader will realize this and not grudge this little word of explanation. I know I would be very glad to read anything the reader ever wrote, and I hope the reader will make the same sort of allowances. If any of the readers would care to send me anything they ever wrote, for criticism or advice, I am always at the Café du Dôme any afternoon, talking about Art with Harold Stearns and Sinclair Lewis, and the reader can bring his stuff along with him, or he can send it to me care of my bank, if I have a bank. Now, if the reader is ready – and understand, I don't want to rush the reader any – we will go back to Yogi Johnson. But please remember that, while we have gone back to Yogi Johnson, Scripps O'Neil and his wife are on their way to the beanery. What will happen to them there I don't know. I only wish the reader could help me.)

PART THREE

Men in War and the Death of Society

It may be likewise noted that affectation does not imply an absolute negation of those qualities which are affected; and therefore, though, when it proceeds from hypocrisy, it be nearly allied to deceit; yet when it comes from vanity only, it partakes of the nature of ostentation: for instance, the affectation of liberality in a vain man differs visibly from the same affectation in the avaricious, for though the vain man is not what he would appear, or hath not the virtue he affects, to the degree he would be thought to have it; yet it sits less awkwardly on him than on the avaricious man, who is the very reverse of what he would seem to be.

HENRY FIELDING

Chapter 11

Yogi Johnson walked out of the workmen's entrance of the pump-factory and down the street. Spring was in the air. The snow was melting, and the gutters were running with snow-water. Yogi Johnson walked down the middle of the street, keeping on the as yet unmelted ice. He turned to the left and crossed the bridge over Bear River. The ice had already melted in the river and he watched the swirling brown current. Below, beside the stream, buds on the willow brush were coming out green.

It's a real chinook wind, Yogi thought. The foreman did right to let the men go. It wouldn't be safe keeping them in a day like this. Anything might happen. The owner of the factory knew a thing or two. When the chinook blew, the thing to do was to get the men out of the factory. Then, if any of them were injured, it was not on him. He didn't get caught under the Employer's Liability Act. They knew a thing or two, these big pump-manufacturers. They were smart, all right.

Yogi was worried. There was something on his

mind. It was spring, there was no doubt of that now, and he did not want a woman. He had worried about it a lot lately. There was no question about it. He did not want a woman. He couldn't explain it to himself. He had gone to the Public Library and asked for a book the night before. He looked at the librarian. He did not want her. Somehow, she meant nothing to him. At the restaurant where he had a meal ticket he looked hard at the waitress who brought him his meals. He did not want her, either. He passed a group of girls on their way home from high school. He looked carefully at all of them. He did not want a single one. Decidedly something was wrong. Was he going to pieces? Was this the end?

Well, Yogi thought, women are gone, perhaps, though I hope not; but I still have my love of horses. He was walking up the steep hill that leads up from the Bear River out onto the Charlevoix road. The road was not really so steep, but it felt steep to Yogi, his legs heavy with the spring. In front of him was a grain and feed store. A team of beautiful horses were hitched in front of the feed store. Yogi went up to them. He wanted to touch them. To reassure himself that there was something left. The nigh horse looked at him as he came near. Yogi put his hand in his pocket for a lump of sugar. He had no sugar. The horse put its ears back and showed its teeth. The other horse jerked its head away. Was this all that his love of horses brought him? After all, perhaps there was something wrong with these horses. Perhaps they had glanders or spavin. Perhaps something had been caught in the tender frog of their hoof. Perhaps they were lovers.

Yogi walked on up the hill and turned to the left onto the Charlevoix road. He passed the last houses of the outskirts of Petoskey and came out onto the open country road. On his right was a field that stretched to Little Traverse Bay. The blue of the bay opening out into the big Lake Michigan. Across the bay the pine hills behind Harbor Springs. Beyond, where you could not see it, Cross Village, where the Indians lived. Even further beyond, the Straits of Mackinac with St Ignace, where a strange and beautiful thing had once happened to Oscar Gardner, who worked beside Yogi in the pump-factory. Further beyond, the Soo, both Canadian and American. There the wilder spirits of Petoskey sometimes went to drink beer. They were happy then. 'Way, 'way beyond, and, in the other direction, at the foot of the lake was Chicago, where Scripps O'Neil had started for on the eventful night when his first marriage had become a marriage no longer. Near there Gary, Indiana, there were the great steel mills. Near there Hammond, Indiana. Near there Michigan City, Indiana. Further beyond, there would be Indianapolis, Indiana, where Booth Tarkington lived. He had the wrong dope, that fellow. Further down there would be Cincinnati, Ohio. Beyond that, Vicksburg, Mississippi. Beyond that, Waco, Texas. Ah! there was grand sweep to this America of ours.

Yogi walked across the road and sat down on a pile of logs, where he could look out over the lake. After all, the war was over and he was still alive.

There was a chap in that fellow Anderson's book

61

that the librarian had given him at the library last night. Why hadn't he wanted the librarian, anyway? Could it be because he thought she might have false teeth? Could it be something else? Would a little child ever tell her? He didn't know. What was the librarian to him, anyway?

This chap in the book by Anderson. He had been a soldier, too. He had been at the front two years, Anderson said. What was his name? Fred Something. This Fred had thoughts dancing in his brain – horror. One night, in the time of the fighting, he went out on parade – no, it was patrol – in No Man's Land, and saw another man stumbling along in the darkness and shot him. The man pitched forward dead. It had been the only time Fred consciously killed a man. You don't kill men in war much, the book said. The hell you don't, Yogi thought, if you're two years in the infantry at the front. They just die. Indeed they do, Yogi thought. Anderson said the act was rather hysterical on Fred's part. He and the men with him might have made the fellow surrender. They had all got the jimjams. After it happened they all ran away together. Where the hell did they run to? Yogi wondered. Paris?

Afterward, killing this man haunted Fred. It's got to be sweet and true. That was the way the soldiers thought, Anderson said. The hell it was. This Fred was supposed to have been two years in an infantry regiment at the front.

A couple of Indians were passing along the road, grunting to themselves and to each other. Yogi called to them. The Indians came over.

'Big white chief got chew of tobacco?' asked the first Indian.

'White chief carry liquor?' the second Indian asked.

Yogi handed them a package of Peerless and his pocket flask.

'White chief heap big medicine,' the Indians grunted.

'Listen,' Yogi Johnson said. 'I am about to address to you a few remarks about the war. A subject on which I feel very deeply.' The Indians sat down on the logs. One of the Indians pointed at the sky. 'Up there gitchy Manitou the Mighty,' he said.

The other Indian winked at Yogi. 'White chief no believe every goddam thing he hear,' he grunted.

'Listen,' Yogi Johnson said. And he told them about the war.

War hadn't been that way to Yogi, he told the Indians. War had been to him like football. American football. What they play at the colleges. Carlisle Indian School. Both the Indians nodded. They had been to Carlisle.

Yogi had played centre at football and war had been much the same thing, intensely unpleasant. When you played football and had the ball, you were down with your legs spread out and the ball held out in front of you on the ground; you had to listen for the signal, decode it, and make the proper pass. You had to think about it all the time. While your hands were on the ball the opposing centre stood in front of you, and when you passed the ball he brought his hand up smash into your face and grabbed you with the other hand under

63

the chin or under your armpit, and tried to pull you forward or shove you back to make a hole he could go through and break up the play. You were supposed to charge forward so hard you banged him out of the play with your body and put you both on the ground. He had all the advantage. It was not what you would call fun. When you had the ball he had all the advantage. The only good thing was that when he had the ball you could rough-house *him*. In this way things evened up and sometimes even a certain tolerance was achieved. Football, like the war, was unpleasant; stimulating and exciting after you had attained a certain hardness, and the chief difficulty had been that of remembering the signals. Yogi was thinking about the war, not the army. He meant combat. The army was something different. You could take it and ride with it or you could buck the tiger and let it smash you. The army was a silly business, but the war was different.

Yogi was not haunted by men he had killed. He knew he had killed five men. Probably he had killed more. He didn't believe men you killed haunted you. Not if you had been two years at the front. Most of the men he had known had been excited as hell when they had first killed. The trouble was to keep them from killing too much. It was hard to get prisoners back to the people that wanted them for identification. You sent a man back with two prisoners; maybe you sent two men back with four prisoners. What happened? The men came back and said the prisoners were knocked out by the barrage. They would give the prisoner a poke in the seat of the pants with a bayonet, and when the prisoner jumped they would say, 'You would run, you son of a bitch,' and let their gun off in the back of his head. They wanted to be sure they had killed. Also they didn't want to go back through any damn barrage. No, sir. They learned those kind of manners from the Australians. After all, what were those Jerries? A bunch of goddam Huns. 'Huns' sounded like a funny word now. All this sweetness and truth. Not if you were in there two years. In the end they would have softened. Got sorry for excesses and begun to store up good deeds against getting killed themselves. But that was the fourth phase of soldiering, the gentling down.

In a good soldier in the war it went like this: First, you were brave because you didn't think anything could hit you, because you yourself were something special, and you knew that you could never die. Then you found out different. You were really scared then, but if you were a good soldier you functioned the same as before. Then after you were wounded and not killed, with new men coming on, and going through your old processes, you hardened and became a good hard-boiled soldier. Then came the second crack, which is much worse than the first, and then you began doing good deeds, and being the boy Sir Philip Sidney, and storing up treasures in heaven. At the same time, of course, functioning always the same as before. As if it were a football game.

Nobody had any damn business to write about it, though, that hadn't at least known about it from hearsay. Literature has too strong an effect on people's minds. Like this American writer Willa Cather, who wrote a book about the war where all the last part of it was taken from the action in the *Birth of a Nation*, and ex-servicemen wrote to her from all over America to tell her how much they liked it.

One of the Indians was asleep. He had been chewing tobacco, and his mouth was pursed up in sleep. He was leaning on the other Indian's shoulder. The Indian who was awake pointed at the other Indian, who was asleep, and shook his head.

'Well, how did you like the speech?' Yogi asked the Indian who was awake.

'White chief have heap much sound ideas,' the Indian said. 'White chief educated like hell.'

'Thank you,' Yogi said. He felt touched. Here among the simple aborigines, the only real Americans, he had found that true communion. The Indian looked at him, holding the sleeping Indian carefully that his head might not fall back upon the snow-covered logs.

'Was white chief in the war?' the Indian asked.

'I landed in France in May 1917,' Yogi began.

'I thought maybe white chief was in the war from the way he talked,' the Indian said. 'Him,' he raised the head of his sleeping companion up so the last rays of the sunset shone on the sleeping Indian's face, 'he got V.C. Me I got D.S.O. and M.C. with bar. I was major in the Fourth C.M.R.'s.'

'I'm glad to meet you,' Yogi said. He felt strangely humiliated. It was growing dark. There was a single line of sunset where the sky and the water met 'way out on Lake Michigan. Yogi watched the narrow line of the sunset grow darker red, thin to a mere slit, and then fade. The sun was down behind the lake. Yogi stood up from the pile of logs. The Indian stood up too. He awakened his companion, and the Indian who had been sleeping stood up and looked at Yogi Johnson.

'We go to Petoskey to join Salvation Army,' the larger and more wakeful Indian said.

'White chief come too,' said the smaller Indian, who had been asleep.

'I'll walk in with you,' Yogi replied. Who were these Indians? What did they mean to him?

With the sun down, the slushy road was stiffening. It was freezing again. After all, maybe spring was not coming. Maybe it did not make a difference that he did not want a woman. Now that the spring was perhaps not coming there was a question about that. He would walk into town with the Indians and look for a beautiful woman and try and want her. He turned down the now frozen road. The two Indians walked by his side. They were all bound in the same direction.

Chapter 12

Through the night down the frozen road the three walked into Petoskey. They had been silent walking along the frozen road. Their shoes broke the new-formed crusts of ice. Sometimes Yogi Johnson stepped through a thin film of ice into a pool of water. The Indians avoided the pools of water.

They came down the hill past the feed store, crossed the bridge over the Bear River, their boots ringing hollowly on the frozen planks of the bridge, and climbed the hill that led past Dr Rumsey's house and the Home Tea-room up to the pool-room. In front of the pool-room the two Indians stopped.

'White chief shoot pool?' the big Indian asked.

'No,' Yogi Johnson said. 'My right arm was crippled in the war.'

'White chief have hard luck,' the small Indian said. 'Shoot one game Kelly pool.'

'He got both arms and both legs shot off at Ypres,' the big Indian said in an aside to Yogi. 'Him very sensitive.'

'All right,' Yogi Johnson said. 'I'll shoot one game.'

They went into the hot, smoke-filled warmth of the pool-room. They obtained a table and took down cues from the wall. As the little Indian reached up to take down his cue Yogi noticed that he had two artificial arms. They were brown leather and both buckled at the elbow. On the smooth green cloth, under the bright electric lights, they played pool. At the end of an hour and a half, Yogi Johnson found that he owed the little Indian four dollars and thirty cents.

'You shot a pretty nice stick,' he remarked to the small Indian.

'Me not shoot so good since the war,' the small Indian replied.

'White chief like to drink a little?' asked the larger Indian.

'Where do you get it?' asked Yogi. 'I have to go to Cheboygan for mine.'

'White chief come with red brothers,' the big Indian said.

They left the pool-table, placed their cues in the rack on the wall, paid at the counter, and went out into the night.

Along the dark streets men were sneaking home. The frost had come and frozen everything stiff and cold. The chinook had not been a real chinook, after all. Spring had not yet come, and the men who had commenced their orgies were halted by the chill in the air that told them the chinook wind had been a fake. That foreman, Yogi thought, he'll catch hell tomorrow. Perhaps it had all been engineered by the pump-manufacturers to get the foreman out of his job. Such things were done. Through the dark of the night men were sneaking home in little groups.

The two Indians walked on either side of Yogi. They turned down a side street, and all three halted before a building that looked something like a stable. It was a stable. The two Indians opened the door and Yogi followed them inside. A ladder led upstairs to the floor above. It was dark inside the stable, but one of the Indians lit a match to show Yogi the ladder. The little Indian climbed up first, the metal hinges of his artificial limbs squeaking as he climbed. Yogi followed him, and the other Indian climbed last, lighting Yogi's way with matches. The little Indian knocked on the roof where the ladder stopped against the wall. There was an answering knock. The little Indian knocked in answer, three sharp knocks on the roof above his head. A trap-door in the roof was raised, and they climbed up through into the lighted room.

In one corner of the room there was a bar with a brass rail and tall spitoons. Behind the bar was a mirror. Easy-chairs were all around the room. There was a pool-table. Magazines on sticks hung in a line on the wall. There was a framed autographed portrait of Henry Wadsworth Longfellow on the wall draped in the American flag. Several Indians were sitting in the easy-chairs reading. A little group stood at the bar.

'Nice little club, eh?' An Indian came up and shook hands with Yogi. 'I see you almost every day at the pump-factory.'

He was a man who worked at one of the machines

near Yogi in the factory. Another Indian came up and shook hands with Yogi. He also worked in the pump-factory.

'Rotten luck about the chinook,' he said.

'Yes,' Yogi said. 'Just a false alarm.'

'Come and have a drink,' the first Indian said.

'I'm with a party,' Yogi answered. Who were these Indians, anyway?

'Bring them along too,' the first Indian said. 'Always room for one more.'

Yogi looked around him. The two Indians who had brought him were gone. Where were they? Then he saw them. They were over at the pool-table. The tall refined Indian to whom Yogi was talking followed his glance. He nodded his head in understanding.

'They're woods Indians,' he explained apologetically. 'We're most of us town Indians here.'

'Yes, of course,' Yogi agreed.

'The little chap has a very good war record,' the tall refined Indian remarked. 'The other chap was a major too, I believe.'

Yogi was guided over to the bar by the tall refined Indian. Behind the bar was the bartender. He was a Negro.

'How would some Dog's Head ale go? asked the Indian.

'Fine,' Yogi said.

'Two Dog's Heads, Bruce,' the Indian remarked to the bartender. The bartender broke into a chuckle.

'What are you laughing at Bruce?' the Indian asked.

The Negro broke into a shrill haunting laugh.

'I knowed it, Massa Red Dog,' he said. 'I knowed you'd ordah dat Dog's Head all the time.'

'He's a merry fellow,' the Indian remarked to Yogi. 'I must introduce myself. Red Dog's the name.'

'Johnson's the name,' Yogi said. 'Yogi Johnson.'

'Oh, we are all quite familiar with your name, Mr Johnson,' Red Dog smiled. 'I would like you to meet my friends Mr Sitting Bull, Mr Poisoned Buffalo, and Chief Running Skunk-Backwards.'

'Sitting Bull's a name I know,' Yogi remarked, shaking hands.

'Oh, I'm not one of those Sitting Bulls,' Mr Sitting Bull said.

'Chief Running Skunk-Backwards's great-grandfather once sold the entire Island of Manhattan for a few strings of wampum,' Red Dog explained.

'How very interesting,' Yogi said.

'That was a costly bit of wampum for our family,' Chief Running Skunk-Backwards smiled ruefully.

'Chief Running Skunk-Backwards has some of that wampum. Would you like to see it?' Red Dog asked.

'Indeed, I would.'

'It's really no different from any other wampum,' Skunk-Backwards explained deprecatingly. He pulled a chain of wampum out of his pocket, and handed it to Yogi Johnson. Yogi looked at it curiously. What a part that string of wampum had played in this America of ours.

'Would you like to have one or two wampums for a keepsake?' Skunk-Backwards asked.

'I wouldn't like to take your wampum,' Yogi demurred.

'They have no intrinsic value really,' Skunk-Backwards explained, detaching one or two wampums from the string.

'Their value is really a sentimental one to Skunk-Backwards's family,' Red Dog said.

'It's damned decent of you, Mr Skunk-Backwards,' Yogi said.

'It's nothing,' Skunk-Backwards said. 'You'd do the same for me in a moment.'

'It's decent of you.'

Behind the bar, Bruce, the Negro bartender, had been leaning forward and watching the wampums pass from hand to hand. His dark face shone. Sharply, without explanation, be broke into high-pitched uncontrolled laughter. The dark laughter of the Negro.

Red Dog looked at him sharply. 'I say, Bruce,' he spoke sharply; 'your mirth is a little ill-timed.'

Bruce stopped laughing and wiped his face on a towel. He rolled his eyes apologetically.

'Ah can't help it, Massa Red Dog. When I seen Mistah Skunk-Backhouse passin' dem wampums around I jess couldn't stand it no longa. Whad he wan sell a big town like New Yawk foh dem wampums for? Wampums! Take away yoah wampums!'

'Bruce is an eccentric,' Red Dog explained, 'but he's a corking bartender and a good-hearted chap.'

'Youah right theah, Massa Red Dog,' the bartender leaned forward. 'I'se got a heart of puah gold.'

'He is an eccentric, though,' Red Dog apologized. 'The house committee are always after me to get another bartender, but I like the chap, oddly enough.'

'I'm all right, boss,' Bruce said. 'It's just that when I see something funny I just have to laff. You know I don' mean no harm, boss.'

'Right enough, Bruce,' Red Dog agreed. 'You are an honest chap.'

Yogi Johnson looked about the room. The other Indians had gone away from the bar, and Skunk-Backwards was showing the wampum to a little group of Indians in dinner dress who had just come in. At the pool-table the two woods Indians were still playing. They had removed their coats, and the light above the pool-table glinted on the metal joints in the little woods Indian's artificial arms. He had just run the table for the eleventh consecutive time.

'That little chap would have made a pool-player if he hadn't had a bit of hard luck in the war,' Red Dog remarked. 'Would you like to have a look about the club?' He took the check from Bruce, signed it, and Yogi followed him into the next room.

'Our committee room,' Red Dog said. On the walls were framed autographed photographs of Chief Bender, Francis Parkman, D.H. Lawrence, Chief Meyers, Stewart Edward White, Mary Austin, Jim Thorpe, General Custer, Glenn Warner, Mabel Dodge, and a full-length oil painting of Henry Wadsworth Longfellow.

Beyond the committee room was a locker room with a small plunge bath or swimming-pool. 'It's really ridiculously small for a club,' Red Dog said. 'But it makes a comfortable little hole to pop into when the evenings are dull.' He smiled. 'We call it the wigwam, you know. That's a little conceit of my own.'

'It's a damned nice club,' Yogi said enthusiastically.

'Put you up if you like,' Red Dog offered. 'What's your tribe?'

'What do you mean?'

'Your tribe. What are you – Sac and Fox? Jibway? Cree, I imagine.'

'Oh,' said Yogi. 'My parents came from Sweden.'

Red Dog looked at him closely. His eyes narrowed. 'You're not having me on?'

'No. They either came from Sweden or Norway,' Yogi said.

'I'd have sworn you looked a bit on the white side,' Red Dog said. 'Damned good thing this came out in time. There'd have been no end of scandal.' He put his hand on his head and pursed his lips. 'Here, you,' he turned suddenly and gripped Yogi by the vest Yogi felt the barrel of an automatic pushed hard against his stomach. 'You'll go quietly through the club-room, get your coat and hat and leave as though nothing had happened. Say polite good-by to anyone who happens to speak to you. And never come back. Get that, you Swede.'

'Yes,' said Yogi. 'Put up your gun. I'm not afraid of your gun.'

'Do as I say,' Red Dog ordered. 'As for those two pool-players that brought you here, I'll soon have them out of this.'

Yogi went into the bright room, looked at the bar, where Bruce, the bartender, was regarding him, got his hat and coat, said good-night to Skunk-Backwards, who asked him why he was leaving so early, and the outside trap-door was swung up by Bruce. As Yogi started down the ladder the Negro burst out laughing. 'I knowed it,' he laughed. 'I knowed it all de time. No Swede gwine to fool ole Bruce.'

Yogi looked back and saw the laughing black face of the Negro framed in the oblong square of light that came through the raised trap-door. Once on the stable floor, Yogi looked around him. He was alone. The straw of the old stable was stiff and frozen under his feet, where had he been? Had he been in an Indian club? What was it all about? Was this the end?

Above him a slit of light came in the roof. Then it was blocked by two black figures, and there was the sound of a kick, a blow, a series of thuds, some dull, some sharp, and two human forms came crashing down the ladder. From above floated the dark, haunting sound of black Negro laughter.

The two woods Indians picked themselves up from the straw and limped towards the door. One of them, the little one, was crying. Yogi followed them out into the cold night. It was cold. The night was clear. The stars were out.

'Club no damn good,' the big Indian said. 'Club heap no damn good.'

The little Indian was crying. Yogi, in the starlight, saw that he had lost one of his artificial arms.

'Me no play pool no more,' the little Indian sobbed.

76

He shook his one arm at the window of the club, from which a thin slit of light came. 'Club heap goddam hell no good.'

'Never mind,' Yogi said. 'I'll get you a job in the pump-factory.'

'Pump-factory, hell,' the big Indian said. 'We all go join Salvation Army.'

'Don't cry,' Yogi said to the little Indian. 'I'll buy you a new arm.'

The little Indian went on crying. He sat down in the snowy road. 'No can play pool me no care about nothing,' he said.

From above them, out of the window of the club came the haunting sound of a Negro laughing.

AUTHOR'S NOTE TO THE READER

In case it may have any historical value, I am glad to state that I wrote the foregoing chapter in two hours directly on the typewriter, and then went out to lunch with John Dos Passos, whom I consider a very forceful writer, and an exceedingly pleasant fellow besides. This is what is known in the provinces as log-rolling. We lunched on rollmops, Sole Meunière, Civet de Lièvre à la Chez Cocotte, marmelade de pommes, and washed it all down as we used to say (eh, reader?) with a bottle of Montrachet 1919, with the sole, and a bottle of Hospice de Beaune 1919 apiece with the jugged hare. Mr Dos Passos, I believe, shared a bottle of Chambertin with me over the marmelade de pommes (Eng., apple sauce). We drank two vieux marcs, and

77

after deciding not to go to the Café du Dôme and talk about Art we both went to our respective homes and I wrote the following chapter. I would like the reader to particularly remark the way the complicated threads of the lives of the various characters in the book are gathered together, and then held there in that memorable scene in the beanery. It was when I read this chapter aloud to him the Mr Dos Passos exclaimed, 'Hemingway, you have wrought a masterpiece.'

P.S. – FROM THE AUTHOR TO THE READER

It is at this point, reader, that I am going to try and get that sweep and movement into the book that shows that the book is really a great book. I know you hope just as much as I do, reader, that I will get this sweep and movement because think what it will mean to both of us. Mr H.G. Wells, who has been visiting at our home (we're getting along in the literary game, eh, reader?) asked us the other day if perhaps our reader, that's you, reader – just think of it, H.G. Wells talking about you right in our home. Anyway, H.G. Wells asked us if perhaps our reader would not think too much of this story was autobiographical. Please, reader, just get that idea out of your head. We have lived in Petoskey, Mich., it is true, and naturally many of the characters are drawn from life as we lived it. But they are other people, not the author. The author only comes into the story in these little notes. It is true that before starting this story we spent twelve years studying the various Indian dialects of the North, and there is still preserved in the museum at Cross Village our translation of the New Testament into Ojibway. But you would have done the same thing in our place, reader, and I think if you think it over you will agree with us on this. Now to get back to the story. It is meant in the best spirit of friendship when I say that you have no idea, reader, what a hard chapter this is going to be to write. As a matter of fact, and I try to be frank about these things, we will not even try and write it until tomorrow.

PART FOUR

The Passing of a Great Race and the Making and Marring of Americans

But perhaps it may be objected to me, that I have against my own rules introduced vices, and of a very black kind, into this work. To which I shall answer: first, that is very difficult to pursue a series of human actions, and keep clear from them. Secondly, that the vices to be found here are rather the accidental consequences of some human frailty or foible, than causes habitually existing in the mind. Thirdly, that they are never set forth as the objects of ridicule, but detestation. Fourthly, that they are never the principal figure at that time on the scene: and lastly, they never produce the intended evil.

HENRY FIELDING

Chapter 13

Yogi Johnson walked down the silent street with his arm around the little Indian's shoulder. The big Indian walking along beside them. The cold night. The shuttered houses of the town. The little Indian, who has lost his artificial arm. The big Indian, who was also in the war. Yogi Johnson, who was in the war too. The three of them walking, walking, walking. Where were they going? Where could they go? What was there left?

Suddenly under a street light that swung on its drooping wire above a street corner, casting its light down on the snow, the big Indian stopped. 'Walking no get us nowhere,' he grunted. 'Walking no good. Let white chief speak. Where we go, white chief?'

Yogi Johnson did not know. Obviously, walking was not the solution of their problem. Walking was all right in its way. Coxey's Army. A horde of men, seeking work, pressing on toward Washington. Marching men, Yogi thought. Marching on and on and where were they getting? Nowhere. Yogi knew it only too well. Nowhere. No damn where at all.

'White chief speak up,' the big Indian said.

'I don't know,' Yogi said. 'I don't know at all.' Was this what they had fought the war for? Was this what it was all about? It looked like it. Yogi standing under the street light. Yogi thinking and wondering. The two Indians in their mackinaw coats. One of the Indians with an empty sleeve. All of them wondering.

'White chief no speak?' the big Indian said.

'No.' What could Yogi say? What was there to say?

'Red brother speak?' asked the Indian.

'Speak out,' Yogi said. He looked down at the snow. 'One man's as good as another now.'

'White chief ever go to Brown's Beanery?' asked the big Indian, looking into Yogi's face under the are light.

'No.' Yogi felt all in. Was this the end? A beanery. Well, a beanery as well as any other place. But a beanery. Well, why not? These Indians knew the town. They were ex-service men. They both had splendid war records. He knew that himself. But a beanery.

'White chief come with red brothers.' The tall Indian put his arm under Yogi's arm. The little Indian fell into step. 'Forward to the beanery.' Yogi spoke quietly. He was a white man, but he knew when he had enough. After all, the white race might not always be supreme. This Moslem revolt. Unrest in the East. Trouble in the West. Things looked black in the South. Now this condition of things in the North. Where was it taking him? Where did it all lead? Would it help him to want a woman? Would spring ever come? Was it worth while after all? He wondered.

The three of them striding along the frozen streets of Petoskey. Going somewhere now. En route.

Huysmans wrote that. It would be interesting to read French. He must try it sometime. There was a street in Paris named after Huysmans. Right around the corner from where Gertrude Stein lived. Ah, there was a woman! Where were her experiments in words leading her? What was at the bottom of it all? All that in Paris. Ah, Paris. How far it was to Paris now. Paris in the morning. Paris in the evening. Paris at night. Paris in the morning again. Paris at noon, perhaps. Why not? Yogi Johnson striding on. His mind never still.

All three of them striding together. The arms of those that had arms linked through each other's arms. Red men and white men walking together. Something had brought them together. Was it the war? Was it fate? Was it accident? Or was it just chance? These questions struggled with each other in Yogi Johnson's brain. His brain was tired. He had been thinking too much lately. On still they strode. Then, abruptly, they stopped.

The little Indian looked up at the sign. It shone in the night outside the frosted windows of the beanery. BEST BY TEST.

'Makeum heap big test,' the little Indian grunted.

'White man's beanery got heap fine T-bone steak,' the tall Indian grunted. 'Take it from red brother.' The Indians stood a little uncertainly outside the door. The tall Indian turned to Yogi. 'White chief got dollars?'

'Yes, I've got money,' Yogi answered. He was prepared to go the route. It was no time to turn back now. 'The feed's on me, boys.'

'White chief nature's nobleman,' the tall Indian grunted.

'White chief rough diamond,' the little Indian agreed.

'You'd do the same for me,' Yogi deprecated. After all, perhaps it was true. It was a chance he was taking. He had taken a chance in Paris once. Steve Brodie had taken a chance. Or so they said. Chances were taken all over the world every day. In China, Chinamen were taking chances. In Africa, Africans. In Egypt, Egyptians. In Poland, Poles. In Russia, Russians. In Ireland, Irish. In Armenia –

'Armenians no take chances,' the tall Indian grunted quietly. He had voiced Yogi's unspoken doubt. They were a canny folk these red men.

'Not even in the rug game?'

'Red brother think not,' the Indian said. His tones carried conviction to Yogi. Who were these Indians? There was something back of all this. They went into the beanery.

AUTHOR'S NOTE TO READER

It was at this point in the story, reader, that Mr F Scott Fitzgerald came to our home one afternoon, and after remaining for quite a while suddenly sat down in the fireplace and would not (or was it could not, reader?) get up and let the fire burn something else so as to keep the room warm. I know, reader, that these things sometimes do not show in a story, but, just the same, they are happening, and think what they mean to chaps like you and me in the literary game. If you should think this part of the story is not as good as it might have been remember, reader, that day in and day out all over the world things like this are happening. Need I add, reader, that I have the utmost respect for Mr Fitzgerald, and let anybody else attack him and I would be the first to spring to his defense! And that includes you too, reader, though I hate to speak out bluntly like this, and take the risk of breaking up a friendship of the sort that ours has gotten to be.

P.S. To the Reader

As I read that chapter over, reader, it doesn't seem so bad. You may like it. I hope you will. And if you do like it, reader, and the rest of the book as well, will you tell your friends about it, and try and get them to buy the book just as you have done? I only get twenty cents on each book that is sold, and while twenty cents is not much nowadays still it will mount up to a lot if two or three hundred thousand copies of the book are sold. They will be, too, if every one likes the book as much as you and I do, reader. And listen, reader. I meant it when I said I would be glad to read anything you wrote. That wasn't just talk. Bring it along and we will go over it together. If you like, I'll re-write bits of it for you. I don't mean that in any critical sort of way either. If there is anything you do not like in this book just write to Mr Scribner's Sons at the home office. They'll change it for you. Or, if you would rather, I will change it myself. You know what I think of you, reader. And you're not angry or upset about what I said about Scott Fitzgerald either, are you? I hope not. Now I am going to write the next chapter. Mr Fitzgerald is gone and Mr Dos Passos had gone to England, and I think I can promise you that it will be a bully chapter. At least, it will be just as good as I can write it. We both know how good that can be, if we read the blurbs, eh, reader?

Chapter 14

Inside the beanery. They are all inside the beanery. Some do not see the others. Each are intent on themselves. Red men are intent on red men. White men are intent on white men or on white women. There are no red women. Are there no squaws any more? What has become of the squaws? Have we lost our squaws in America? Silently, through the door which she had opened, a squaw came into the room. She was clad only in a pair of worn moccasins. On her back was a papoose. Beside her walked a husky dog.

'Don't look!' the drummer shouted to the women at the counter.

'Here! Get her out of here!' the owner of the beanery shouted. The squaw was forcibly ejected by the Negro cook. They heard her thrashing around in the snow outside. Her husky dog was barking.

'My God! What that might have led to!' Scripps O'Neil mopped his forehead with a napkin.

The Indians watched with impassive faces. Yogi Johnson had been unable to move. The waitresses had covered their faces with napkins or whatever was handy. Mrs Scripps had covered her eyes with *The American Mercury*. Scripps O'Neil was feeling faint and shaken. Something had stirred inside him, some vague primordial feeling, as the squaw had come into the room.

'Wonder where that squaw came from?' the drummer asked.

'Her my squaw,' the little Indian said.

'Good God, man! can't you clothe her?' Scripps O'Neil said in a dumb voice. There was a note of terror in his words.

'Her no like clothes,' the little Indian explained. 'Her woods Indian.'

Yogi Johnson was not listening. Something had broken inside of him. Something had snapped as the squaw came into the room. He had a new feeling. A feeling he thought had been lost for ever. Lost for always. Lost. Gone permanently. He knew now it was a mistake. He was all right now. By the merest chance he had found it out. What might he not have thought if that squaw had never come into the beanery? What black thoughts he had been thinking! He had been on the verge of suicide. Self-destruction. Killing himself. Here in this beanery. What a mistake that would have been. He knew now. What a botch he might have made of life. Killing himself. Let spring come now. Let it come. It couldn't come fast enough. Let spring come. He was ready for it.

'Listen,' he said to the two Indians. 'I want to tell you about something that happened to me in Paris.'

The two Indians leaned forward. 'White chief got the floor,' the tall Indian remarked.

'What I thought was a very beautiful thing happened to me in Paris,' Yogi began. 'You Indians know Paris? Good. Well, it turned out to be the ugliest thing that ever happened to me.'

The Indians grunted. They knew their Paris.

'It was the first day of my leave. I was walking along the Boulevard Malesherbes. A car passed me and a beautiful woman leaned out. She called to me and I came. She took me to a house, a mansion rather, in a distant part of Paris, and there a very beautiful thing happened to me. Afterward someone took me out a different door than I had come in by. The beautiful woman had told me that she would never, that she could never, see me again. I tried to get the number of the mansion but it was one of a block of mansions all looking the same.

'From then on all through my leave I tried to see that beautiful lady. Once I thought I saw her in the theatre. It wasn't her. Another time I caught a glimpse of what I thought was her in a passing taxi and leaped into another taxi and followed. I lost the taxi. I was desperate. Finally on the next to the last night of my leave I was so desperate and dull that I went with one of those guides that guarantee to show you all of Paris. We started out and visited various places. 'Is this all you've got?' I asked the guide.

' "There is a real place, but it's very expensive," the guide said. We compromised on a price finally, and the guide took me. It was in an old mansion. You looked

91

through a slit in the wall. All around the wall were people looking through slits. There, looking through slits could be seen the uniforms of men of all the Allied countries, and many handsome South Americans in evening dress. I looked through a slit myself for a while nothing happened. Then a beautiful woman came into the room with a young British officer. She took off her long fur coat and her hat and threw them into a chair. The officer was taking off his Sam Browne belt. I recognized her. It was the lady whom I had been with when the beautiful thing happened to me.' Yogi Johnson looked at his empty plate of beans. 'Since then,' he said, 'I have never wanted a woman. How I have suffered I cannot tell. But I've suffered, boys, I've suffered. I blamed it on the war. I blamed it on France. I blamed it on the decay of morality in general. I blamed it on the younger generation. I blamed it here. I blamed it there. Now I am cured. Here's five dollars for you, boys.' His eyes were shining. 'Get some more food to eat. Take a trip somewhere. This is the happiest day of my life.'

He stood up from his stool before the counter, shook the one Indian impulsively by the hand, rested his hand for a minute on the other Indian's shoulder, opened the door of the beanery, and strode out into the night.

The two Indians looked at one another. 'White chief heap nice fella,' observed the big Indian.

'Think him was in the war?' asked the little Indian.

'Me wonder,' the big Indian said.

'White chief said he buy me new artificial arm,' the little Indian grumbled.

'Maybe you get more than that,' the big Indian said.

'Me wonder,' the little Indian said. They went on eating.

At the other end of the counter of the beanery a marriage was coming to an end.

Scripps O'Neil and his wife sat side by side. Mrs Scripps knew now. She couldn't hold him. She had tried and failed. She had lost. She knew it was a losing game. There was no holding him now. Mandy was talking again. Talking. Talking. Always talking. That interminable stream of literary gossip that was bringing her, Diana's, marriage to an end. She couldn't hold him. He was going. Going. Going away from her. Diana sitting there in misery. Scripps listening to Mandy talking. Mandy talking. Talking. Talking. The drummer, an old friend now, the drummer, sitting reading his Detroit *News*. She couldn't hold him. She couldn't hold him. She couldn't hold him.

The little Indian got up from his stool at the beanery counter, and went over to the window. The glass on the window was covered with thick rimy frost. The little Indian breathed on the frozen windowpane, rubbed the spot bare with the empty sleeve of his mackinaw coat and looked out into the night. Suddenly he turned from the window and rushed out into the night. The tall Indian watched him go, leisurely finished his meal, took a toothpick, placed it between his teeth, and then he too followed his friend out into the night.

Chapter 15

They were alone in the beanery now. Scripps and Mandy and Diana. Only the drummer was with them. He was an old friend now. But his nerves were on edge tonight. He folded his paper abruptly and started for the door.

'See you all later,' he said. He went out into the night. It seemed the only thing to do. He did it.

Only three of them in the beanery now. Scripps and Mandy and Diana. Only those three. Mandy was talking. Leaning on the counter and talking. Scripps with his eyes fixed on Mandy. Diana made no pretense of listening now. She knew it was over. It was all over now. But she would make one more attempt. One more last gallant try. Perhaps she still could hold him. Perhaps it had all been just a dream. She steadied her voice and then she spoke.

'Scripps, dear,' she said. Her voice shook a little. She steadied it.

'What's on your mind?' Scripps asked abruptly. Ah there it was. That horrid clipped speech again.

'Scripps, dear, wouldn't you like to come home?'

Diana's voice quavered. 'There's a new *Mercury*.' She had changed from the London *Mercury* to *The American Mercury* just to please Scripps. 'It just came. I wish you felt like coming home, Scripps, there's a splendid thing in this *Mercury*. Do come home, Scripps, I've never asked anything of you before. Come home, Scripps! Oh, won't you come home?'

Scripps looked up. Diana's heart beat faster. Perhaps he was coming. Perhaps she was holding him. Holding him. Holding him.

'Do come, Scripps, dear,' Diana said softly. 'There's a wonderful editorial in it by Mencken about chiropractors.'

Scripps looked away.

'Won't you come, Scripps?' Diana pleaded.

'No,' Scripps said. 'I don't give a damn about Mencken any more.'

Diana dropped her head. 'Oh, Scripps,' she said. 'Oh, Scripps.' This was the end. She had her answer now. She had lost him. Lost him. Lost him. It was over. Finished. Done for. She sat crying silently. Mandy was talking again.

Suddenly Diana straightened up. She had one last request to make. One thing she would ask him. Only one. He might refuse her. He might not grant it. But she would ask him.

'Scripps,' she said.

'What's the trouble?' Scripps turned in irritation. Perhaps, after all, he was sorry for her. He wondered.

'Can I take the bird, Scripps?' Diana's voice broke.

'Sure,' said Scripps. 'Why not?'

Diana picked up the bird-cage. The bird was asleep. Perched on one leg as on the night when they had first met. What was it he was like? Ah, yes. Like an old osprey. An old, old osprey from her own Lake Country. She held the cage to her tightly.

'Thank you, Scripps,' she said. 'Thank you for this bird.' Her voice broke. 'And now I must be going.'

Quietly, silently, gathering her shawl around her, clutching the cage with the sleeping bird and the copy of *The Mercury* to her breast, with only a backward glance, a last glance at him who had been her Scripps, she opened the door of the beanery, and went out into the night. Scripps did not even see her go. He was intent on what Mandy was saying. Mandy was talking again.

'That bird she just took out,' Mandy was saying.

'Oh, did she take a bird out?' Scripps asked. 'Go on with the story.'

'You used to wonder about what sort of bird that was,' Mandy went on.

'That's right,' Scripps agreed.

'Well that reminds me of a story about Gosse and the Marquis of Buque,' Mandy went on.

'Tell it, Mandy. Tell it,' Scripps urged.

'It seems a great friend of mine, Ford, you've heard me speak of him before, was in the marquis's castle during the war. His regiment was billeted there and the marquis, one of the richest if not the richest man in England, was serving in Ford's regiment as a private. Ford was sitting in the library one evening. The library was a most extraordinary place. The walls were made of

96

bricks of gold set into tiles or something. I forget exactly how it was.'

'Go on,' Scripps urged. 'It doesn't matter.'

'Anyhow, in the middle of the wall of the library was a stuffed flamingo in a glass case.'

'They understand interior decorating, these English,' Scripps said.

'Your wife was English, wasn't she?' asked Mandy.

'From the Lake Country,' Scripps answered. 'Go on with the story.'

'Well, anyway,' Mandy went on, 'Ford was sitting there in the library one evening after mess when the butler came in and said: "The Marquis of Buque'a compliments and might he show the library to a group of friends with whom he has been dining?" They used to let him dine out and sometimes they let him sleep in the castle. Ford said, "Quite," and in came the marquis in his private's uniform followed by Sir Edmund Gosse and Professor Whatsisname, I forget it for the moment, from Oxford. Gosse stopped in front of the stuffed flamingo in the glass case and said, "What have we here, Buque?"

'"It's a flamingo, Sir Edmund," the marquis answered.

'"That's not my idea of a flamingo," Gosse remarked.

'"No, Gosse. That's God's idea of a flamingo," Professor Whatsisname said. I wish I could remember his name.'

'Don't bother,' Scripps said. His eyes were bright. He leaned forward. Something was pounding inside of him. Something he could not control. 'I love you, Mandy,' he said. 'I love you. You are my woman.' The thing was pounding away inside of him. It would not stop.

'That's all right,' Mandy answered. 'I've known you were my man for a long time. Would you like to hear another story? Speaking of woman.'

'Go on,' Scripps said. 'You must never stop, Mandy. You are my woman now.'

'Sure,' Mandy agreed. 'This story is about when Knut Hamsun was a streetcar conductor in Chicago.'

'Go on,' Scripps said. 'You are my woman now, Mandy.'

He repeated the phrase to himself. My woman. My woman. You are my woman. She is my woman. It is my woman. My woman. But, somehow, he was not satisfied. Somewhere, somehow, there must be something else. Something else. My woman. The words were a little hollow now. Into his mind, though he tried to thrust it out, there came again the monstrous picture of the squaw as she strode silently into the room. That squaw. She did not wear clothes, because she did not like them. Hardy, braving the winter nights. What might not the spring bring? Mandy was talking. Mandy talking on in the beanery. Mandy telling her stories. It grows late in the beanery. Mandy talks on. She is his woman now. He is her man. But is he her man? In Scripps's brain that vision of the squaw. The squaw that strode unannounced into the beanery. The squaw who had been thrown out into the snow. Mandy talking on. Telling literary reminiscences.

Authentic incidents. They had the ring of truth. But were they enough? Scripps wondered. She was his woman. But for how long? Scripps wondered. Mandy talking on in the beanery. Scripps listening. But his mind straying away. Straying away. Straying away. Where was it straying? Out into the night. Out into the night.

Chapter 16

Night in Petoskey. Long past midnight. Inside the beanery a light burning. The town asleep under the Northern moon. To the North the tracks of the G.R.&I. Railroad running far into the North. Cold tracks, stretching North toward Mackinaw City and St Ignace. Cold tracks to be walking on at this time of night.

North of the frozen little Northern town a couple walking side by side on the tracks. It is Yogi Johnson walking with the squaw. As they walk Yogi Johnson silently strips off his garments. One by one he strips off his garments, and casts them beside the track. In the end he is clad only in a worn pair of pump-makers shoes. Yogi Johnson, naked in the moonlight, walking North beside the squaw. The squaw striding along beside him. She carries the papoose on her back in his bark cradle. Yogi attempts to take the papoose from her. He would carry the papoose. The husky dog whines and licks at Yogi Johnson's ankles. No, the squaw would carry the papoose herself. On they stride. Into the North. Into the Northern night.

Behind them come two figures. Sharply etched in the moonlight. It is the two Indians. The two woods Indians. They stoop and gather up the garments Yogi Johnson has cast away. Occasionally, they grunt to one another. Striding softly along in the moonlight. Their keen eyes not missing a single cast-off garment. When the last garment has been cast off they look and see far ahead of them the two figures in the moonlight. The two Indians straighten up. They examine the garments.

'White chief snappy dresser,' the tall Indian remarks, holding up an initialled shirt.

'White chief going get pretty cold,' small Indian remarks. He hands a vest to the tall Indian. The tall Indian rolls all the clothing, all the cast-off garments, into a bundle, and they start back along the tracks to the town.

'Better keep clothes for white chief or sellem Salvation Army?' asks the short Indian.

'Better sellem Salvation Army,' the tall Indian grunts. 'White chief may never come back.'

'White chief come back all right,' grunted the little Indian.

'Better sellem Salvation Army, anyway,' grunts the tall Indian. 'White chief need new clothes, anyhow, when spring comes.'

As they walked down the tracks toward town, the air seemed to soften. The Indians walk uneasily now. Through the tamaracks and cedars beside the railway tracks a warm wind is blowing. The snow-drifts are melting now beside the tracks. Something stirs inside the two Indians. Some urge. Some strange pagan disturbance.

The warm wind is blowing. The tall Indian stops, moistens his finger and holds it up in the air. The little Indian watches. 'Chinook?' he asks.

'Heap chinook,' the tall Indian says. They hurry on toward town. The moon is blurred now by clouds carried by the warm chinook wind that is blowing.

'Want to get in town before rush,' the tall Indian grunts.

'Red brothers want be well up in line,' the little Indian grunts anxiously.

'Nobody work in factory now,' the tall Indian grunted.

'Better hurry.'

The warm wind blows. Inside the Indians strange longings were stirring. They knew what they wanted. Spring at last was coming to the frozen little Northern town. The two Indians hurried along the track.

THE END

Well, reader, how did you like it? It took me ten days to write it. Has it been worth it? There is just one place I would like to clear up. You remember back in the story where the elderly waitress, Diana, tells about how she lost her mother in Paris, and woke up to find herself with a French general in the next room? I thought perhaps you might be interested to know the real explanation of that. What actually happened was that her mother was taken violently ill with the bubonic plague in the night, and the doctor who was called diagnosed the case and warned the authorities. It was the day that the great exposition was to be opened, and think what a case of bubonic plague would have done for the exposition as publicity. So the French authorities simply had the woman disappear. She died toward morning. The general who was summoned and who then got into bed in the same room where the mother had been, always seemed to us like a pretty brave man. He was one of the big stockholders in the exposition, though, I believe. Anyway, reader, as a piece of secret history it always seemed to me like an awfully good story, and I know you would rather have me explain it here than drag an explanation into the novel, where really, after all, it has no place. It is interesting to observe, though, how the French police hushed the whole matter up, and how quickly they got a hold of the coiffeur and the cab-driver. Of course, what it shows is that when you're travelling abroad alone, or even with your mother, you simply cannot be too careful. I hope it is all right about bringing this in here, but I just felt I owed it to you, reader, to give some explanation. I do not believe in these protracted good-bys any more than I do in long engagements, so I will just say a simple farewell and Godspeed, reader, and leave you now to your own devices.

To Have and Have Not

Ernest Hemingway

Harry Morgan was hard – the classic Hemingway hero – rum-running and man-running from Cuba to the Florida Keys during the dismal days of the Depression. He ran risks, too, stray coast-guard bullets and sudden double-crosses, but it was the only way he could keep his boat, keep his independence and keep his belly full . . .

'Absorbing and moving. It opens with a fusillade of bullets, reaches its climax with another, and sustains a high pitch of excitement throughout'
Times Literary Supplement

'Its tragic scenes are rendered with an economy of words and a power that might well be the despair of a lesser writer'
Scotsman

'This active, passionate life on the verge of the tropics is perfect material for the Hemingway style, and the reader carries away from the book a sense of freshness and exhilaration; trade winds, southern cities and warm seas all admirably described by the instrument of precision with which he writes'
New Statesman

arrow books

A Farewell to Arms

Ernest Hemingway

In 1918 Ernest Hemingway enlisted to fight in the 'war to end all wars'. He volunteered for ambulance service in Italy, was wounded and twice decorated. Out of his experiences came *A Farewell To Arms*.

In an unforgettable depiction of war, Hemingway recreates the fear, the comradeship, the courage of his young American volunteers, and the men and women he encounters along the way with conviction and brutal honesty. A love story of immense drama and uncompromising passion *A Farewell To Arms* is a testament to Hemingway's unique and unflinching views of the world and the people around him.

'A novel of great power'
Times Literary Supplement

'Hard, almost metallic, glittering, blinding by the reflections of its hard surface, utterly free of sentimentality'
Arnold Bennett

'A most beautiful, moving and humane book'
Vita Sackville-West

The First Forty-Nine Stories

Ernest Hemingway

A collection of Hemingway's first forty-nine short stories, featuring an introduction by the author, and lesser known as well as familiar tales, including 'Up in Michigan', 'Fifty Grand', and 'The Light of the World', and the *Snows of Kilimanjaro*, *Winner Take Nothing* and *Men Without Women* collections.

'There are many kinds of stories in this book. I hope you will find some that you like . . . In going where you have to go, and doing what you have to do, and seeing what you have to see, you dull and bend the instrument you write with. But I would rather have it bent and dulled and know I had to put it on the grindstone and hammer it into shape and put a whetstone to it, and know that I had something to write about, than to have it bright and shining and nothing to say, or smooth and well-oiled in the closet, but unused'
Ernest Hemingway, from his Preface

'Mr Hemingway, applying that quick eye and wrist of his to the rings of the boxer and bull-fighter, achieves some unforgettable reporting of the world in which blood is argument . . . The author's exceptional gift of narrative quality gives the excitement of a well-told tale to what is, in fact, a simple description of a scene'
Guardian

arrow books

For Whom the Bell Tolls

Ernest Hemingway

High in the pine forests of the Spanish Sierra, a guerrilla band prepares to blow up a vital bridge. Robert Jordan, a young American volunteer, has been sent to handle the dynamiting. There, in the mountains, he finds the dangers and the intense comradeship of war. And there he discovers Maria, a young woman who has escaped from Franco's rebels.

For Whom The Bell Tolls is Hemingway's finest novel, a passionate evocation of the pride and the tragedy of the Civil War that tore Spain apart.

'The best book Hemingway has written'
New York Times

'The best fictional report on the Spanish Civil War that we possess'
Anthony Burgess

'One of the greatest novels which our troubled age will produce'
Observer

arrow books

Men Without Women

Ernest Hemingway

Men Without Women was a milestone in Hemingway's career. *Fiesta* had already established him as a novelist of exceptional power, but with these short stories, his second collection, he showed that it is possible, within the space of a few pages, to recreate a scene with absolute truth, bringing to life details observed only by the eye of a uniquely gifted artist.

Hemingway's men are bullfighters and boxers, hired hands and hard drinkers, gangsters and gunmen. Each of their stories deals with masculine toughness unsoftened by woman's hand. Incisive, hard-edged, pared down to the bare minimum, they are classic Hemingway territory.

'Painfully good . . . no-one can deny their brilliance'
The Nation

arrow books

ALSO AVAILABLE IN ARROW

The Old Man and the Sea

Ernest Hemingway

'The best short story Hemingway has written . . . no page of this
beautiful master-work could have been done better or differently'
Sunday Times

Set in the Gulf Stream off the coast of Havana, Hemingway's
magnificent fable is the story of an old man, a young boy and a
giant fish. In a perfectly crafted story, which won for Hemingway
the Nobel Prize for Literature, is a unique and timeless vision of
the beauty and grief of man's challenge to the elements in which
he lives.

'It is unsurpassed in Hemingway's oeurve. Every word tells and
there is not a word too many'
Anthony Burgess

'A quite wonderful example of narrative art. The writing is as taut,
and at the same time as lithe and cunningly played out, as
the line on which the old man plays the fish'
Guardian

arrow books